# You **WILL** Believe in Love

## Homer Starkey

Aventine Press

Published by Aventine Press
55 East Emerson St.
Chula Vista CA, 92101
www.aventinepress.com

ISBN: 978-1-59330-824-7
Library of Congress Control Number: 2013909463
Library of Congress Cataloging-in-Publication Data
You WILL Believe in Love / Homer Starkey

Printed in the United States of America

*for Annie*

|PART ONE| October 2002

# Chapter 1

Pot Callin' Kettle Diner — Deepwater, Texas

No ring on her left hand.

Okay, she wasn't married, but she probably had a boyfriend. A boyfriend that probably didn't appreciate the way she looked in those tight black yoga pants that just barely kept her ass cleavage concealed as she maneuvered between tables, picking up empty coffee cups and plates with half-eaten orders of biscuits and gravy.

No, her boyfriend didn't, couldn't appreciate that ass. Or that bosom—that natural high bosom that moved ever so gently as she moved.

And she moved.

By God, did she move.

It was the first thing he had noticed—that generous bust, which stretched out and tested every weave of her tight low-cut sweater as she took his order. Clearly, she wore that sweater expressly to stimulate the loins of her male customers.

"One coffee coming right up. Would you like regular or decaf?"

"Yes, very much so . . . Oh, sorry. I was thinking about someth— ugh, I mean, regular, please. Black. Thank you."

Each time she passed him, he opened his mouth slightly to say something but stopped himself. The right words weren't there yet.

Whatever he said had to be perfect, so that she'd remember it for years to come. It had to be genuine, yet slightly corny. And most of all, the delivery had to be right: confident, yet slightly embarrassed.

He had to wait for the appropriate time. She couldn't be busy attending to minutiae. She couldn't be distracted by irate thoughts about some impatient patron whom she was growing to loathe more and more each time he asked for the ETA of his chicken-fried steak.

He had to have her undivided attention. He had to wait for her lips to form a smile or her eyes to reveal an opportunity—or better yet, both.

And he had to get that boyfriend of hers out of his mind. Surely, she probably had one. He knew the odds, and they were high. But on or off the market, at very least, she would appreciate his awkward-yet-memorable line. Maybe she and her boyfriend might even have a laugh about it later that night before they went to bed.

And then maybe she would see him again months later, perhaps after a messy breakup with said boyfriend, and his odd pick-up line would resound in her head, and she would say hello, how are you, didn't we, weren't you the guy . . . And things would fall into place then.

No, this could still work out. A much worse scenario—the worst, really—would be that she had no husband, no boyfriend, or any significant other: she had an unrequited love.

Here was the really scary thing: he might not ever know about the unrequited love. He might marry this girl and shake hands with the unrequited love at the wedding reception. He might see the unrequited love kiss his bride slowly on the cheek and whisper something in her ear and never think anything of it. She might look longingly at the unrequited love as he walks away, while he, her groom, goes off to dance with his new mother-in-law. Maybe she'll shed a few tears as their plane taxies off to the runway, finally cleared to whisk them off to their Hawaii honeymoon, and when he leans in and asks her what's wrong, she'd say "nothing" or "I'm just so happy," and he'd recline back into his airplane seat, his oblivious mind already occupied with the lack of leg room.

That odious possibility almost closed his mouth for good as she came toward him again, but when she nodded at his empty coffee cup and asked if he needed a refill, smiling with both her mouth and her beautiful hazel-green eyes, he knew he had the perfect line, the one that would address all concerns at once, and asked with confident embarrassment:

"Are you in love with someone?"

"Excuse me?" asked the waitress, furrowing her lovely brow.

Not the response he was looking for. He could ask again, but her Irish eyes were definitely no longer smiling.

"Oh, sorry," he started. "I just thought . . ."

Her disapproving look didn't change.

He searched for something, anything, to say.

"Hi!" The forced chirpiness in his voice was painful even for him to hear. "My name is Pal. That's short for Palestrina. I know it's an unusual name. I can tell you the story behind it, if you'd like."

"Uh huh," drawled the waitress. "You know what? My shift's about over, so I'm going to get Cyndi to cover this table, okay?"

"Oh, sure, sure . . . Not a problem. Yeah, it's probably best. Again, real sorry about that. I'll just sit here quietly and drink my coffee."

The last sentence he said more to himself. She was already gone.

The long hand on the plastic clock on the wall kept circling. Between his third and fourth refill, Pal ordered a second cup of coffee, asking the new waitress to set it on the table across from him while trying to avoid looking her in the judgmental eye.

Finally, Gab showed up, a bounce in his stride and an unsolicited "Heya! Howzit goin'?" for everyone he walked past on his way to the booth where Pal sat in solemn silence. It was obvious he had something to tell Pal. He had that bursting-with-things-to-tell-Pal look again.

"OK, remember that primal scream therapy stuff they had a few years back?" he asked in lieu of a hello.

"Yes. It never caught on," Pal replied. He did not like where these conversations usually went, or for that matter, where they took place. The Pot Callin' Kettle was not his idea of a business incubator. But then he recalled that Rod Canion came up with the idea of Compaq Computer Corporation on a napkin at a diner and felt slightly better.

"So what? Doesn't mean it wasn't a good idea," Gab said.

"What makes you so sure you can make it work?" said Pal out of habit as he looked around for the waitress, so that he might wave her down for the check. She was nowhere in sight. Who knows what the first waitress told her.

Gab squirmed excitedly in his seat. Pal's indifference was no impediment to his rambling.

"Tell me: how did you hear about primal scream therapy? No, no, don't answer. It was through people yapping about it, right?"

Gab paused. Pal waited.

"Do I answer now?" he finally asked.

"Yes, it was all through word of mouth," Gab went on. "But I bet that word of mouth didn't tell you where these primal scream therapy classes were being offered, right? And I bet if you had known where to find this class, you would have checked it out, right? At least once? Poked your head in to hear what all the fuss was about?"

Across the room, their new waitress was talking to the one Pal had pissed off earlier. Pal made desperate-to-go puppy eyes her way. She noticed but carried on with her conversation. Pal shifted his focus reluctantly back to his friend.

"So you're saying that primal scream therapy only failed because it wasn't properly marketed?" he asked.

Gab took a big gulp of coffee, grimaced, and pumped his fist in the air, all at the same time.

"Egg-zactly," he said after swallowing the coffee. "Exactly that!"

"Marketing is expensive, Gab."

"On a global scale, yes, I'm inclined to agree, but we are smarter than that. We are going to target a very select demographic."

"We're both up to our asses in debt," Pal said. "Mainly because I keep letting you talk me into less-than-sound investments."

"I know," Gab said. "I really thought for sure the drive-thru grooming place would work out."

"Well, it didn't. And that was the last of the investment money— what little I had left after your hare-brained house-cleaning-slash-home-repair venture. What did you name that one? Oh, yeah, 'Man Maid.' Why did you neglect to mention those two guys you hired were ex-cons you met in a Huntsville icehouse?"

"I believed them to be rehabilitated. I had faith in the Texas penal system."

"*We* almost became part of the Texas penal system! They made off from that house with fifty grand worth of jewelry!"

"And electronics," added Gab. "You gotta admit though: they did a great job fixing the kitchen cabinets."

"Let's not dwell on details," Pal said. "The point is, I always let you talk me into the stupidest—"

"Palestrina! Listen to yourself! Listen to your *anger!* Now, what if you, in your present condition, saw an ad that read: '*Primal Scream Therapy. Let It All Out. Purge Your Demons*' . . ."

"'Purge your demons'?"

"Or whatever. You're the creative one. You really are, you know."

"I'm immune to your flattery," said Pal. Still, his friend's proposal might have something to it. "I guess I could help you with a marketing plan," he added reluctantly. "Work is kind of slow."

Gab took another sip of coffee and scrunched up his face. "Ice cold. This place has really gone downhill. Anyway, I totally understand—I've let you down too many times, there's only so many times a heart can be broken, yada yada . . . Wait a minute. Did you just say yes?"

"Well, not exactly . . ."

Gab slammed down his cup and squirmed in his seat some more.

"That's my boy! We'll find us a space, fix it up nice, and charge local socialites fifty bucks an hour to scream and holler and make complete asses out of themselves. They'll love it!" Gab reached over the table to slap Pal on the shoulder.

"They probably would love it," agreed Pal, digging himself in deeper.

"I know this one is *the* idea." Gab was now bouncing in his seat. "It's going to be huge. I'm telling you. You can quit your job as a Web master or whatever, and I can stop with these stupid temp jobs."

"Web designer," sighed Pal.

"Yeah, that's what I thought. Well, mister designer, you can design us a site. What do you say? So much to gain, nothing to lose, very little overhead," Gab said.

"That's not true. Renting a space alone would run us at least—"

"Stop! Don't dwell on the details! Remember that Earl Nightingale CD you made me listen to?"

"That was a mistake, I think," Pal muttered.

"Remember what he said? 'We become what we think about.'"

Pal sighed again. He was feeling an overpowering desire to excuse himself to the restroom and climb out the window.

"Come on, tell me you're in," pleaded Gab. "I don't want to do this without you."

"You *can't* do this without me."

Gab stopped squirming.

"I know that," he said softly. "You don't think I know that? Tell me you're in. Come on, Pal. You're the only one who understands. You're the only one who gets it."

"God damn it," Pal whispered. Gab took it as an affirmative.

"Yes!" he said, pumping his fist in the air again.

"Okay, okay. But Gab? This is it. If this doesn't work out, you're getting a steady job."

"Sure, sure. Now let's get out of here and get to work! Where's our waitress?"

Pal pointed her out. She was still across the room and talking to the goddess in the tight sweater.

"Wow," Gab said.

"No, the other one."

"Ugh," Gab said. "Oh well. That good-looking one probably has a boyfriend." He stuck his hand high in the air and waved. "Hey darlin'! Check!"

# Chapter 2

Sumner Residence — West University, Houston, Texas

Pal and Gab first met during late registration at the University of Houston. Pal had originally planned to attend UT Austin with his high school girlfriend. They had visited the campus many times during their senior year and spent a few weekends exploring the hip capital of Texas together.

A week after high school graduation, Pal's girl decided to move there early and take a summer course. She fell in love with the Austin live music scene, and it wasn't long before she fell in love with someone *from* the Austin live music scene. Left high and dry, Pal moped at home as he waited around for the fall semester to begin, until he realized he didn't have it in him to take that trek up Highway 290 again. U of H, his backup school, would have to do.

He was standing in the registration line, still confused and heartbroken, when the guy directly in front of him turned around and struck up a conversation. Pal tried to use body language to indicate that he was not in a talkative mood, but his efforts were in vain.

". . . but everyone calls me Gab—because I talk a lot," Gab said at the end of a long ramble, delivered in one breath, about U of H girls, morning classes and the ungodliness of their hour, a man's need for sleep, some philosopher whose name Pal recalled only dimly, some indie band Pal had never heard of at all, and the U of H girls again.

"No kidding," Pal said. "Nice to meet you, Gab. I'm Pal. Short for Palestrina."

"Palestrina? That's a name?" Gab asked. "Sounds Italian. You Italian?"

"Nope."

"Where you from?"

"Deepwater."

"No shit? Me, too!"

And that's when Gab made an enthusiastic suggestion—the first one of many in the course of their friendship—that they carpool to Houston. Pal was reluctant at first, certain that he would regret saying yes to this hyperactive weirdo, but finally agreed. With textbook costs being what they were, it was only sensible to save a little gas money.

The episode turned out to be the beginning of a counterintuitive but beautiful friendship. Pal sometimes felt like a basset hound trying to keep up with a beagle.

It was a mystery to him why Gab bothered with college. He hardly attended his classes, opting instead to roam about the campus and get distracted by girls, who often found him charming enough to distract him further. Still, somehow he got by each semester, content with a 2.2 grade point average.

When Gab's mother died, less than a year after her husband's fatal heart attack, Gab disappeared. Several days later, a very relieved Pal found him in the middle of the Rothko Chapel—noticeably thinner, stinking to high heavens, unshaved, puffy-eyed, and attempting to meditate.

"I can't do it. I can't do it. I can't . . ." Gab repeated under his breath as Pal helped him up off of the floor and dragged him to his car. Thirty minutes later, they were at Pal's apartment in Deepwater, where Gab proceeded to use up all the hot water in the course of a forty-minute shower.

After a few days' regular meals at the Pot Callin' Kettle under Pal's close supervision, Gab started to look better. After a few weeks, he resumed lifting weights at the gym. In a month's time, he was actually completing school projects. He also began to stay up until the early hours of the morning reading Zen Buddhist texts, like *The Gateless Gate* and *Zen Flesh, Zen Bones*. It was the first time in the three years of their friendship that Pal saw Gab so focused and, dare he say, spiritual.

Pal ended up changing his major from Marketing to English Literature, partly because of the way Gab went on about the program, and partly because his marketing courses were boring him stiff. If even the slacker ADD poster boy Gab could be captivated by *Beowulf* and *Bleak House* deeply enough to raise his GPA to a respectable 3.0, maybe Pal was missing out on a good thing. Also, there was no shortage of attractive coeds in the cozy discussion circles.

The night after their graduation ceremony, he and Gab went to McEwan's Pub to celebrate their freedom. It had taken them both six years to get a Bachelor of Arts in English Literature—a distressing fact but not a surprising one, since Pal had switched majors halfway into his junior year, and Gab consistently dropped out of every third course he signed up for. Regardless, a bender was long overdue. Both of them were eager to quit thinking critically about things for a while, especially their job prospects, armed as they were with B.A.s in English.

"We coo' be ed'tors," Pal tried to enunciate.

"Nah, I want an editor to work for me. I'm going to be a writer," Gab said. High tolerance for cheap Irish whiskey gave his elocution a tremendous edge.

"Buh you don' wry . . ."

"You don't know everything about me, brother. As a matter of fact, I write all the time. I love it."

"How you gun make a livin'?"

"There are always ways. You just need a foot in the door, and I have just the foot in mind. Remember Trisha?"

Pal did not.

"Redhead? Tits out to here? A mellifluous voice as loud as the horns of Jericho? We dated briefly freshman year—after I broke up with Brenda, but before I got with that Asian TA, what's her name . . ."

Now Pal remembered.

"Well, ol' Trish is an actress now, in New York City, no less! Not Broadway, of course, not yet, but moderately successful. She's in some play about vaginas, I think, or some other crazy shit. Anyway, she's agreed to give one of my plays to her producer boyfriend. It pays to stay friends with your exes."

"Haf t' piss," Pal slurred before getting up, falling down, getting back up, and staggering into the ladies room.

Gab refused the offer of another pint from the waitress when she came to the table.

"Someone has to give directions to the cab driver," he explained. He wondered how Pal was making out in the women's restroom. He had yet to exit.

His attention shifted across the room, where a handful of loud rugby players from Rice were guzzling Guinness and throwing darts everywhere but at the actual dartboard.

A girl sat at the table next to them, drawing something quietly in a big black book.

Before he was even aware of it, Gab had walked over to her.

"You with these guys?"

"No, I'm just sketching them. They don't mind."

"That must be a heck of a task. They are an awfully wobbly bunch." Gab leaned in closer. "Would you mind coming over to sit next to me at my table? It's quieter, and frankly, I fear for your safety around these fellows. A friend of mine lost an eye in this very spot a month ago because of a rogue dart. He was an artist like you, only he was working in watercolor. After the incident, he lost his depth perception, and his art suffered. He blamed me for his predicament. Said I should have kept him abreast of the danger."

"I'm engaged."

"If you mean engaged in your drawing, I will leave you alone. I respect the artist's right to create undisturbed. But if you mean you are engaged to be married, I assure you I'm just looking for a friend. I just lost one, remember?"

Gab and Marisa did not start sleeping together until well after her marriage. After each indiscretion, she told herself this was the last time. But Gab was like a bad habit.

Eventually, she put her foot down, demanding they return to being just friends, without benefits. So when Gab called her and asked to meet up for something other than their usual pastime, she saw no harm in inviting him over.

They now sat next to one another on a large leather couch in the den of the house she shared with her husband, Dr. Phil Sumner. The doctor was out, attending some fund-raising event for his hospital. Marisa was trying to follow Gab's unnecessarily round-about and long-winded explanation of his new business idea.

After he finally ran out of words, she offered her opinion.

"It's an okay idea, I guess. I've heard about primal scream therapy before. Is this really what you want to do, though? Why not do something more constructive? You have so much talent. What about putting your English degree to good use? Maybe teach kids?"

"What could be more constructive than helping people purge their fears and anxieties?" he said. "This isn't a scam, Marisa—it's a legitimate therapeutic method. And it's not going to be easy money, either—it'll take hard work, especially from Pal. We have to advertise. We have overhead to think about. It's really quite daunting. We could use an investor."

"Don't give me that look. My husband would never go for it."

"Come on," Gab said. "Surely you can convince him with your wifely wiles."

"Why don't *you* try to convince him yourself? You've got wiles to burn."

"He doesn't like me. I think he senses that I'm competition."

Marisa rolled her eyes.

"You know, you roll your eyes almost as perfectly as you roll your r's," Gab said, smiling.

"That joke got old the fifth time around. And don't change the subject—there is no competition," she said. "He thinks you're gay."

"You told him that I was gay?"

"No, but I didn't deny it when he asked."

Gab laughed.

"Smart! Way to throw him off the scent of another man between his sheets. Good way to score us more alone time, too. 'Marisa, where were you last night? I know you only got back at midnight.' 'Oh, just out shoe shopping with Gab. We stayed out afterwards drinking chocolate martinis and singing show tunes at a karaoke bar.' Brilliant ploy."

"Actually, he asked me if you were gay after he first met you. I wasn't sure myself yet, so that's what I told him."

"What? How could you doubt my masculinity?"

"It was before we started having sex." Marisa shrugged. "And besides, a homosexual doesn't have to be effeminate. You could be straight-acting and still be gay."

"Straight-*acting*? I hit on you at a bar!"

"Funny, I remember you saying you were only looking for a friend."

"I just said that to get inside your defense perimeter." Gab wiggled his eyebrows.

"Well, like it or not, we're just friends now."

"Okay, okay. I'll drop it."

"Don't get pissy. We agreed it was a bad idea, remember?"

"Uh huh," Gab said, thinking of something else. "So, if we can't talk your well-respected, and more importantly, well-paid heart surgeon husband into investing—"

"Not a chance. Not even going to try."

"Got it. Well, what about your studio?"

"What about it?"

"Do you think we could use the studio space for the sessions? Just until we start making enough money to rent our own place? You hardly even use it anymore."

"It's kind of a mess . . ."

"No biggie. Pal and I will clean it up."

He leaned in closer to Marisa. "Please?" he whispered piteously into her ear.

"Let me think about it."

Unable to resist, he nuzzled her neck and was just about to kiss it when Marisa pushed him away gently.

"Gab, no."

"I miss you," he said, reaching around her waist and pulling her closer to him.

"It's only been a couple of weeks."

"Without you, that's a lifetime."

"He'll be home soon."

"I won't stay long."

# Chapter 3

Lutheran Hospital — Medical Center, Houston, Texas

The walls of the treatment room were covered with accolades and awards, and even laminated newspaper clippings attesting to the excellence of Dr. Sumner, interventional cardiologist.

Pal reached for a framed journal article, taking note of the doctor's stoic, tight-lipped headshot as he removed the frame from the wall for closer inspection.

Phi Beta Kappa graduate. Distinguished alumnus of the Baylor College of Medicine. Recipient of the Award of Merit from the American Heart Association. On the board of directors for the National Heart Association. Elected Fellow of the Royal Society of Medicine of the United Kingdom. And Pal supposed being the lead author of a book on cardiovascular medicine counted for something, too. It was plain to see why his physician recommended *this* guy.

Last week, during a routine physical, Pal let it slip that he had been having minor chest pains off and on for about a year. No big deal, he said. Probably anxiety. But his doctor, perhaps fearful of being sued, would have none of it and sent him right away to a specialist. He couldn't detect anything himself, he said, but when it came to the heart, better safe than sorry. And now here Pal was, waiting for someone to tell him the results of the previous session's MRI, EKG, and other tests with acronyms he couldn't remember.

*Well, if something's wrong, this Sumner hotshot will surely find it.*

Pal thought back to the first time he felt the pain in his chest. It was a few days after his fiancée gave him back the engagement ring.

She had stared at the ring for a few seconds before sliding it across the dining room table toward him. He must have looked confused. Her face was blank.

Pal had glanced around the furniture store, feeling like all the other customers were watching them. He and his fiancée had sat down at the table they picked out from a catalog. It was a cheap and plain-looking thing, off-white parawood, but they were on a budget: the wedding was going to cost a pretty penny. Besides, they would probably trade up after they bought a house, maybe give it to Gab along with their other starter furniture. They couldn't live in her apartment forever, after all. She had reminded him of this several times just in the past week alone.

But now this had happened.

"Baby, what are you doing?" Pal had asked, but he knew what she was doing.

"I'm leaving you. I'm breaking off our engagement. Please, don't take this too hard."

"How am I supposed to take it?"

If ever he had thought this moment would come, he damn sure didn't think it would come in an IKEA showroom.

She had been dropping not-so-subtle hints of her displeasure with their financial state for a while now, like flipping through Neiman Marcus and Nordstrom catalogs and sighing loudly. But he lived in denial of her unhappiness, convincing himself that she was patiently waiting for his Web design business to take off.

When she started to go out in the evenings without him, he became afraid that she would meet someone new.

But this fear turned out to be unfounded. The other man was not someone new.

"Remember the time I told you about my old crush? The boxer?"

"The guy you described as a 'fighter, not a lover'?"

"Well, actually I couldn't have known then. He was just an infatuation. I guess what I meant to say was he would rather fight than—"

"Fuck."

Pal stood up from the table he was not going to buy on his almost maxed-out credit card.

"God, Pally, why do you have to be so crass? All I meant was that he used to be too wrapped up in his career to really have time for me. Now he's retired from boxing. He made quite a name for himself in the ring, and he's parlayed that into a successful business. He sells gym equipment and training DVDs now."

A matronly patron squeezed herself with some difficulty into the chair Pal vacated, grumbling about its comfort, or rather lack thereof. Then she saw the ring in the center of the table, its solitaire diamond glittering under the fluorescent overhead light.

"Is this your ring, dear?" she asked the girl who did not want to marry Pal after all.

"No, I'm afraid it isn't," she answered without hesitation.

The lady's pudgy hand extended toward the ring. Pal snatched it before she could reach it, and she drew her hand back quickly and huffed in disapproval. Pal apologized, walked out of the store, got into his car, and drove away in no particular direction.

Three days after his fiancée told him she was leaving him to go twelve rounds with another man, Pal drove back to Deepwater. When he walked into his apartment, he saw that it was practically empty.

"She even took my goddamn iMac," he said to himself, just before feeling something tighten beneath his sternum. Grabbing his chest, he looked around for a chair to sit on. There was none. Pal fell to one knee.

But this was not the time to obsess over the breakup. To suppress unwelcome thoughts, Pal read Dr. Sumner's credentials for the third time. It didn't help much, so he stood up, hung the frame back on its nail in the wall, and focused his attention on a shiny plastic model of a heart that sat on the counter.

He picked it up to examine it. Before he could get a good grip, it slipped from his hands, fell to the floor, and broke apart.

Dr. Sumner entered the room without the customary tap on the closed door. Pal was still desperately attempting to put the chambers of the model heart back in their correct places.

"You have the left and right ventricles mixed up. Switch them round. They should snap in place."

"Ventricles?"

"Here, allow me."

Pal watched as the cardiologist rebuilt the heart in a matter of seconds. He hoped this was a good sign, despite being prepared for bad news.

"Actually, I could use this model to explain your condition," said Dr. Sumner.

"Oh, great," Pal said. "I have a condition."

Life had taught him that a "condition" was always a bad thing to have. No one ever had good conditions. "His condition is terminal." "Her condition is critical."

"Give it to me straight, doc. I'm ready."

He wasn't ready. He braced himself by holding on to the back of a chair.

Dr. Sumner tried not chuckle.

"So, I've reviewed your test results . . ."

Pal's grip tightened to the point of white knuckles, as if a gale force wind was about to blow him out of the room.

"Both the MRI and the stress echocardiogram indicate that you have something known as hypertrophic cardiomyopathy, HCM for short. This condition means your heart has a thickened septum, which is this wall right here, separating the left and right sides of the heart's chambers." Sumner's fingers caressed the plastic heart in several strategic places. "The thickened septum is obstructing blood flow and causing a backup of blood in your heart, in layman's terms. It's a wonder you haven't been diagnosed until now. HCM is usually detected in childhood."

Dr. Sumner wondered if the patient standing right in front of him heard a word of the diagnosis he just delivered. The young man had his eyes shut tight and wasn't even facing him. Usually his patients at least made direct eye contact at this point. Most of them actually stopped blinking. Some of them would ask him to repeat everything, and perhaps even a third time, and then maybe ask for a graphic representation of the procedure to help digest the information. But this one just stood there.

"So what happens now?" Pal finally asked, opening his eyes and turning his head toward the doctor.

"Well, the good news is that your condition can be treated without invasive surgery. We can perform what is known as alcohol septal ablation. It's a percutaneous procedure: basically, we'd use some ethanol to kill off some of the excess tissue, thin out the muscle, and relieve the obstruction of blood flow."

Dr. Sumner opened up the plastic model of the heart and pointed to the place where Pal's heart muscle had grown so thick it was causing blood to back up.

"Right now, your heart and lungs have to work harder to supply your tissues with oxygen. You probably have been experiencing fatigue, dizziness, mood swings—am I right?"

Pal nodded. He had been intimately acquainted with all three of those practically since birth.

"To be blunt, right now you are at risk of cardiac arrest."

"A heart attack? I might have a heart attack?!"

Pal let go of the chair and grabbed his chest again, then caught himself doing this and placed his hands back on the chair.

"Unfortunately, yes. Like I said, usually this condition is discovered early and treated with medication. Your situation has grown quite a bit more urgent, but don't worry—it's not the end of the world. However, I wouldn't hold off on that procedure any longer than necessary. I'm going to go ahead and schedule you to come in for it next Thursday."

"No way. I need time to think about doing this."

"I assure you, it's a routine procedure. I've performed hundreds of ablations, and only a small percentage ever needs a follow up."

"A small percentage? How small are we talking here?"

"Single digits small. In fact, I'm flying to Prague tomorrow to address the International Surgical Society about my success rate, at their request. So take my advice and relax. Don't worry about a thing. I've been performing and perfecting this procedure for years. I help people live long, productive lives, and I'm going to do the same for you, Palestrina."

The first name was a nice gesture, Pal thought, but ultimately an empty one.

"Look, Doctor Sumner, you have to understand . . . It's my heart, you know? What if you miss something, or, or aim half an inch too high, or—"

Pal stopped talking as Dr. Sumner walked over to the wall and leveled the frame Pal had re-hung on it crookedly. He brushed a bit of dust off of it, then he straightened it again, even though it didn't need it.

"Now, there are some things about the procedure that I must go over with you," he said as he turned back toward Pal and motioned for him to have a seat. Pal let go of the chair and sat down in it.

"First things first. The nature of the procedure is such that when we inject the alcohol into the extra heart muscle, it will induce a heart attack."

Pal felt himself getting woozy.

"Of course, we will give you something for the anxiety and the pain, but it's important for you to know that during the procedure you will remain awake."

Pal was no longer woozy. He was unconscious.

# Chapter 4

Loft Above the White Lightning Bar — Deepwater, Texas

When Gab was fifteen, he read somewhere that Jim Morrison shunned material possessions, and that the Lizard King once bought a coat on a cold San Francisco night only to give it to a homeless man the next afternoon. This inspired young Gab to give away his leather bomber jacket to a homeless schizophrenic he met under the 59 bridge at Shepherd.

Once the television show *21 Jump Street* became popular and he saw how cool Johnny Depp looked in his worn bomber jacket, Gab tried to find the homeless man from under the bridge again, but had no luck. He tried to take comfort in his disappearance by imagining that the man probably moved to someplace with a cooler climate where he couldn't go before, thanks to Gab's selfless gift.

But in general, contempt for creature comforts stayed with Gab, or so he told himself as he paced around his sparsely decorated, tidy, and uncluttered loft.

As he walked in vague circles around this Spartan abode, Gab thought of what questions to pose to the people who answered his ad for a primal scream therapist and who were due to show up any minute. No specific line of inquiry suggested itself. Instead, his mind wandered to the not-so-distant past, when he used to room with Pal.

After graduation, they both struggled to find work. Luckily, rent was cheap in Deepwater, and they were content with a steady diet of peanut butter and jelly sandwiches, punctuated by occasional visits to the all-you-can-eat Chinese buffet.

After spending the better part of a year searching for gainful employment, Pal walked into the Enron building and walked out with a steady job. Initially hired to write copy for crisis communications, Pal gravitated toward desktop publishing and layout design. It was perfect for him. Now he spent his workdays puttering around in Photoshop, airbrushing away Ken Lay's double chin and rubber stamping more hair onto Jeff Skilling's head for their headshots in the annual report, and he wasn't stuck writing the press releases when the company did something wrong. He realized quickly he was no good at corporate doublespeak.

While Pal sat in his cubicle touching up photos of the C-suite executives, Gab got a job at a petroleum plant as a Fire Watch. Gab loved his new position. It entailed watching welders and pipe fitters at work ten hours a day, making sure the sparks from the welds didn't catch the dry grass around everyone on fire.

Gab took the job seriously. It was his first real job, and he wanted to make a good impression. If he played his cards right, maybe someday he could be plant manager. With this in mind, he showed up for work early every day and berated anyone coming in more than a few minutes late. These exchanges usually followed along the lines of:

"Yo! We got work to do today, Roy."

"Yo! Go fuck yourself, Fire Watch."

"Tommy, was there a car wreck or something?"

"Yeah, probably somewhere, Fire Watch."

"Come on, Mani. This is the third time this week."

"What, that I banged your girlfriend, Fire Watch?"

The crew's prayers for Gab's speedy termination were answered one dry day in July, when an ambitious spark caught the tall dead grass around a storage tank on fire.

Gab was talking to Marisa on his cell phone, trying to entice her to his place after work to hang out and watch old movies, oblivious to the quickly spreading fire and the screams of his crew, who were yelling at him to get off his goddamned phone and grab one of the two extinguishers sitting a few feet in front of him.

Finally, Gab noticed the fire.

"Oh shit, oh shit, oh shit," the crew heard him say as he ran past the two fire extinguishers on his way to safer ground.

"That's three strikes, Fire Watch," his supervisor said later as he escorted Gab personally off the plant premises.

"Three? How did I screw up three times?"

"Strike one: using your cell phone on company time. Strike two: putting your crew in harm's way. If Mani hadn't jumped off that man lift and grabbed the extinguisher—hell, I don't want to think about it."

"You know, he's late almost every day," Gab said.

"And strike three: telling me to go fuck myself."

"I've never told you that."

"My word against yours, Fire Watch."

"Really? Well, in that case, go fuck yourself," Gab said as his ex-supervisor closed the gate behind him.

"Bye, Fire Watch."

Gab had the suspicion that "Fire Watch" was just the plant workers' way of saying "asshole."


A few days after his termination, Gab received some more bad news from Pal.

"I'm moving out! We got engaged!"

"What?"

"Yeah! She said yes."

Pal had no idea why such wonderful news made Gab stare at him so blankly.

"Remember? Yesterday? I told you I was going to pop the question at the Waterwall?"

Gab had not been listening at the time. He was already sinking into depression after being let go from the best—the only—job, he'd ever had.

"Where am I supposed to go?" he asked Pal.

"Stay here. The rent is cheap. Or you can get the hell out of Deepwater. This town has seen better days."

"Pal, I got laid off."

"Laid off? So soon?"

"OK, I got fired. I've been trying to forget about it."

"Shit," Pal said.

"I'll survive. Fuck it. Anyway, congratulations, brother."

Pal went on to tell him that he finally got approved for the small business loan for his startup Web design firm, with a little money left over. He was going to put it away for unforeseen business expenses, but he could help Gab out if he needed it. Gab nodded his head slightly.

"Any idea what you're going to do now?" Pal asked.

"I've been thinking of starting a company myself, actually," Gab said. "A bungee store. It will only sell things with bungee cords attached to them. I want to call it 'Everything Bungee.'"

"That's the worst idea I have ever heard."

"I'm just kidding around," said Gab, lying.

The day Pal moved out, Gab looked around their apartment and was suddenly struck with a sense of emptiness. So he piled all his things into his car and headed to the White Lightning Bar, a private club one of his father's old buddies owned in the Deepwater warehouse district.

"Joe, I'm in need of a place to stay. You still have that space upstairs?" he asked the man behind the bar as soon as he walked in. Although there were only a half dozen working light bulbs in the entire establishment, Joe wore dark sunglasses that made him resemble a white-haired Roy Orbison. Gab had never seen him without them on, day or night. For all he knew, Joe could be crossed-eyed.

"Say no more," Joe said, opening the cash register and producing a key to the small loft above the bar. "You know, your father's girlfriend used to live up there."

Gab got the sense that under the sunglasses, the man was winking at him.

He climbed the rest of the stairs to his new home wondering what other secrets his father had kept from the family.

When the people responding to the ad in the back of the *Houston Press* began to arrive, Gab directed them to wait in the main room, which was empty except for a few plastic lawn chairs. He set up his two other chairs, the nice wooden ones, in the kitchen facing one another and called out the first name on his list.

The interviews—five in rapid succession—were accompanied by the bass thump of Clarence Carter's "Strokin'" rising through the floorboards from the jukebox in the bar below. The candidates waiting in the main room tapped their feet unconsciously.

During the interviews, Gab did most of the talking.

"So, you have a psychology degree from Cornell? That's cool. I used to have a girlfriend who had a friend who went to law school there. I don't know if she passed the bar, probably did. I mean, it's a great school, and she was a smart girl. Or at least I heard she was smart—I have no idea if she is, really. My girlfriend thought she was, but that was just her point of view. How do I know if she's right? I went to a self-improvement seminar not long ago, and the guy there said that there are three points of view to every story. So if she tells me that her husband takes her for granted, that's she's just a trophy wife, and that he's sucking the life out of her, that may just be her point of view. Then there's his point of view, which you can't really access, because, well, what are you going to do? Ask him if he's really a huge asshole or if his cheating wife has been telling you tales? Can't do that. And then there's the truth, which is like the third-person omniscient point of view, God's I guess, if we're all really His creatures. And no one can ever see it except Him. Oh well. So, you went to law school? I don't know if that really qualifies you to be a primal scream therapist."

With the next applicant, Gab incorporated his exercise routine of crunches and leg lifts into the interviewing process.

"Veterinarian school? Thirty-four. Texas A&M? Thirty-five. Wow, that is great. Thirty-six. So you work with animals? What number am I on? Thirty-seven? How do you feel about working with people?"

All applicants demonstrated a nice aptitude for screaming, especially applicant number three. Unfortunately, that one had no time for the second round of interviews (to be held immediately following the first round) because he said he had to hurry to make a sperm donation at the fertility clinic on the north side of Houston before it closed for the day.

Gab was sorry to hear it. The candidate had interviewed very well.

Number three's elimination put one person—a stripper named Brandi—ahead of the rest in the first round. Brandi had many questions concerning the nature of the position.

"Yes, yes," explained Gab. "There is a lot of screaming involved. I mean, it is called primal *scream* therapy. But you can dance, too, maybe. I don't know. We could certainly try something. I'm open to suggestions."

After an impromptu lap dance, Gab was optimistic about Brandi's future as his new employee.

The second round of interviews were short and mostly a formality, since Gab knew damned well Brandi was getting the job.

When everyone left, Gab went down to the bar to grab a beer. Joe was leaning on the counter and talking to a nice-looking redhead wearing retro Ray-Ban eyeglasses and a black leather motorcycle jacket. Her hair was pulled back tightly, making her look like a librarian with a sexy, sinister secret.

"A round for the house, on me," Gab said after noticing he, the chick, and some old guy dozing over a beer mug in the corner were the only people in the bar.

"Big money," Joe said.

"Hey! Howzit goin'?" Gab asked the woman at the bar. "Got to say, I like your style."

"Thanks," she replied.

"Didn't expect anyone here so early. This is a 'last stop' kind of place."

"Oh, I just dropped in to see Joe."

Gab turned to look at Joe, who was popping the top off a Lone Star. "Joe, you old devil."

Joe grinned and handed Gab the bottle.

"Don't get your hopes up, or mine. She and I used to do a little business together, didn't we, gorgeous? Here you go. Shirley Temple." Joe placed the glass in front of the woman.

"I was hoping to get him to rent me the loft upstairs, but it looks like that is out of the question, with you living up there. What was with all the people screaming?"

"Interviews. I'm an entrepreneur," said Gab. "I'm getting into the therapy business."

"Therapy? You mean the kind where everybody screams?"

"That's the one. You've heard of primal scream therapy? It's very soothing."

"Didn't sound too soothing to me."

Gab smiled and took a swig of his lager. He liked this girl.

"Are you going to have your sessions up there?" she asked.

"No, I've got a studio. Just have to get it ready."

Gab proceeded to describe his plan to the red-haired beauty in detail. She listened, never interrupting him, not even when he went off on a few tangents.

"So, what were you looking to do with my loft?" Gab said when he was done. "That is, if it hadn't been *my* loft?"

"Just looking for a new work space. I'm in the therapy business too, you might say."

"Really? What kind?"

"Let's just say, in my line of work, you also get the occasional screamer."

# Chapter 5

Lucky You All Chinese Restaurant & Lunch Buffet — Deepwater, Texas

Pal liked his restaurants clean and quiet. Lucky You All (or as the locals called it, "Lucky Y'all") was one of those restaurants: so clean you could eat the food straight off the table and so quiet you could hear yourself swallowing your green tea.

He was finishing his third cup when he saw Gab's car pull up into the empty pothole-ridden parking lot. No one in Deepwater went to Lucky Y'all for dinner, not when they charged twice as much for the same food. (Also, what? No buffet after 2 p.m.?)

Gab walked in and sat down across from him, as giddy as a Catholic schoolgirl who had snuck a kiss from her BFF's hunky older brother.

"What's up?"

"I'm in trouble," Pal said with a slightly overdone groan that had served him well for nearly two decades.

"Women trouble?" asked Gab, looking around for the waiter.

"No, Gab," Pal sighed. "Not all trouble is women trouble." Honestly, Gab should have known by the volume of Pal's groan how serious things were.

"All trouble is women trouble, Pal. Sometimes it's just not a straight line from the woman to the trouble. More of a jagged zigzag. What's wrong?"

"I'm going to be having heart surgery in about a week. Well, not really heart surgery, but a heart procedure . . . thing. It's not pumping right, or pumping enough, or maybe it's pumping to the wrong place. I've got a fucked-up heart, in short. Apparently, I could have a heart attack at any moment."

"And we're eating at this place?" Gab chuckled. "Wouldn't be my choice for a last meal, but hey."

"I'm serious, Gab."

The conversation was not going according to plan. Where were the terse manly words of sympathy, the brotherly shoulder of support?

"Ah, hell. Don't sulk, Pal. My dad had heart surgery, and it was no big thing. A triple bypass, then a quadruple bypass. He was going for some sort of record, I think. You aren't even getting opened up, you lucky son of a bitch. Wait till you have to get your sternum sliced and your ribs pulled back like a baked potato skin."

Pal touched his own chest and grimaced.

"You're not helping me feel better. I might still need that done, if this procedure goes wrong."

"They've perfected all this heart surgery stuff, Pal. Like I said, my dad had loads of them."

"Didn't your father *die* of a heart attack after one of those surgeries?"

"Well, sure," Gab answered, shrugging. "But damn, Pal, he was sixty-seven years old, a chain smoker, a womanizer, and a meat eater. His heart just wore itself out."

"Well, I'm still worried," Pal said, slowly shaking his head and staring down at the table.

"You can worry. I mean, it's normal." Gab suspected he wasn't helping. This frustrated him. He wanted to help.

The waiter came and took their order: steamed vegetables for Pal and spinach dumplings for Gab.

"When's the surgery? Sorry, I mean the procedure?" Gab asked when they were halfway finished.

"In about a week and a half. My surgeon is supposed to be the best in his field. He's going to Prague to blow sunshine up his own ass in front of the world's medical elite. When he gets back, it's go time."

"Hey, you know what's funny? My girlfriend Marisa's husband is a heart surgeon," Gab said before starting to laugh. "Man, what are the odds?"

"Well, with all the girlfriends you've had, I'd say pretty high."

"What's your surgeon's name? I'll find out through her if he's any good."

"Did you hear anything I just said? He's supposed to be the best."

"I'm sure that's what they all say. He's not going to tell you he's only slightly above average, now is he? Or slightly below average, as the case may be?"

"I know this guy is good. He worked on Burt Reynolds."

"Burt Reynolds? Really?" Gab asked.

"I think so." Pal tried to remember the actor Dr. Sumner mentioned. "Maybe it was Patrick Swayze . . . or was it Patrick Swayze's father?"

"Wait, I thought Swayze's father died when he was a boy."

"How could you possibly know that?"

"Remember when Barbara Walters interviewed him, and he cried on camera, and it was such a big deal? He was crying because he never had a chance to tell his dad he really loved him."

"So cliché," Pal said.

Gab banged his fist on the table, making the silverware jump. Pal jumped, too.

"You know what? I bet actors fake crying in those interviews. Maybe their publicists talk them into shedding a few tears to score more press coverage."

"I don't know. Patrick's career has seen better days."

The two friends sat in silence until the tray with the check and fortune cookies came out a few minutes later, with the exception of Gab mumbling, "fucking *To Wong Foo*" and "*Black Dog* wasn't so bad." Then they argued for five minutes over whether you were supposed to read the fortune before or after you ate the fortune cookie.

"Guess what?" said Gab after the cookies were finally eaten. "Our new instructor is meeting us at the Mausoleum later."

Pal hated the Mausoleum. Upon entering that club, he usually morphed into an asshole and stayed in that state until a good night's sleep purged the songs of My Life With The Thrill Kill Cult from his head.

"Gab, I told you, I am not wasting another evening there ever again."

Then he remembered Gab mentioning an instructor a second earlier.

"Wait. You found an instructor?"

Gab grinned.

"How come I wasn't in on this? We don't even have a space yet!"

"Calm down. We have a space, too, thanks to yours truly. It's not much, but it'll do for now. Marisa agreed to let us use her studio on Washington. We just need to fix it up a bit."

"And the instructor?" Pal asked, suspicious.

"I put an ad in the back page of the *Press* a couple weeks back."

"A couple weeks back? And you didn't tell me?"

"I interviewed some people at my place today. Good turnout."

"What if I had said no? You were going to do this whole thing without me?"

"I knew you would say yes," Gab said.

"I thought you were going to be the fool up there telling everyone to yell and go nuts."

"Never considered it."

"No? Okay, let me ask you something. In all your proactive, forward-looking strategizing and planning, did you ever consider how we're going to pay this instructor you hired?"

"Oh, don't worry about that," Gab said.

"You know what? You really missed out. You would have made a great screaming instructor. Shit, all you'd need to do is lock yourself in a room with some people, and they'd all be screaming like banshees in ten minutes."

"No, we are going to take this seriously, and seriously means getting a professional. By the way, this professional wants seventy percent of what we will be pulling in."

"Seventy percent?"

"I know it sounds like a lot, but she can be persuasive, believe me. *More* than persuasive, actually. The best part about it is, she's bringing her own clientele. Now we don't have to worry about advertising costs."

"She has her own clientele?"

"Yep. Been doing this for a while. Built up quite a client list. Twenty, thirty people. She really just needs a new, bigger place to hold her sessions. Her apartment is too small, she says."

"She holds primal scream sessions in an apartment?"

"Well . . . um . . . no."

"So she's not a scream therapist?" Pal asked, confused. "Why did she answer the ad?"

"She didn't, actually. I met her down at Joe's bar. She was asking him if my loft was for rent. Then she told me what she did, and I thought: hey, this is a hell of a lot more lucrative than any primal scream class we could put together. So I worked out a deal with her. Told her we had a studio, and we'd let her use it if we got a percentage. Took some negotiating, but we're all partners now. You and I get 15 percent each of her take. And the best thing is, we don't have to do anything except help her move her things into Marisa's studio."

"Gab," Pal said painfully and slowly. "Is she a therapist of any sort?"

"Well, not exactly."

"What's that mean?"

"She's not exactly a therapist. Not a therapist in the biased I-paid-two-hundred-grand-for-a-psychology-degree sense, no."

"So what the hell is she then?"

"She's a dominatrix."

Pal lowered his head to the table and began to slowly bang his forehead on his crumpled fortune, which read, "Doubt is the beginning, not the end, of wisdom."

# Chapter 6

Sumner Residence — West University, Houston, Texas

Phil Sumner grew up in the dry heat of Phoenix, Arizona. His father was an ambitious and self-assured attorney who rarely had time for his wife and son. Whatever spare hours he got he usually spent sulking in a lonely part of the house with a bottle of Scotch until his emotions got the better of him.

Then he would stagger into the master bedroom where his wife slept and wake her with accusations of infidelity. When he did not get an admission of adultery, he would try to beat it out of her.

On many occasions Phil would hear the commotion in his parents' room. He would hear his mother plead for mercy yet admit nothing. When these domestic disturbances occurred, Phil froze underneath his covers, paralyzed by fear and indecision, until one night when something inside him snapped and he got out of bed.

He entered the master bedroom cautiously. When his father heard the door creak, he let go of his wife's hair, and she fell heavily to the floor. He held a bloody .38 Special in his other hand.

"Your mother's a whore," he told Phil. "You understand?"

Phil was fifteen years old, but facing his drunk, armed father, he felt like a defenseless toddler. He looked past his father to see his mother lying on her back, her face swollen almost beyond recognition. Instinctively, he started to walk toward her, his fear of the man with a gun in his hand forgotten.

"Don't take another step, boy."

Phil stopped moving.

"There is a lot of blood," he said. "Please, I need to help her."

His father said nothing, then, his hand shaking slightly, raised the revolver to his own temple.

"Do it," Phil said, almost whispering. "Fucking do it."

"What's that? Speak up."

"I said do it! Do us all a favor, motherfucker!"

Phil shivered. At that moment, he felt every inch of his skin.

"Sorry, kid. I'm not the one fucking your mother, it would appear," his father said, smiling crookedly. Then he lowered the gun and extended it toward Phil, handle first.

"If I kill myself, you and your mother will not benefit from my life insurance policy," he said. He cocked his head back and laughed, as though he had said something very witty, then motioned with the gun ever so slightly, so that Phil would take it.

Phil stepped slowly toward him and, after some hesitation, took the gun from his hand, pointing it at his father's chest. He thought mainly to keep him at bay, but before he knew it, he was already pulling the trigger. Each time the hammer fell, a click sounded.

Still smiling, Phil's father patted his son's head and walked past him out of the bedroom.

As Phil tended to his mother, he heard a car leave the drive. When she regained consciousness, she refused to go to the hospital.

"We have to get you to the emergency room."

"We can't," Phil's mother said with much effort. "Word will get out."

"People already know."

His mother's tears mixed with drying blood. Phil waited.

"Get my purse. I'll call Dr. White."

The family doctor arrived quickly, considering it was the middle of the night. He came prepared, bringing a bag of medical supplies and sutures. He put seven stitches in Mrs. Sumner's eyebrow and two in the bridge of her nose as Phil looked on. He then cleaned the remaining blood off of her face using hydrogen peroxide and cotton balls.

Many of Dr. White's patients were referred to him by Phil's father. Any accident—car wreck, on-the-job injury, a slip and fall on the wet floor of a grocery store—had Jack Sumner sending people the doctor's way. Dr. White would say whatever was needed to help Sumner's argument, and Sumner would pass him a bit of cash under the table as soon as settlement came.

"Should I call the police?" Phil asked as the doctor packed up.

"The police will do nothing if your mother does not file a report," the doctor said without looking up from his bag. "So no, don't bother calling them."

Phil heard anger in the doctor's voice.

"I would, however, get rid of that gun—and any others that are in the house—as soon as possible, in case your father decides to shoot you, your mother, or himself when he returns home. You know how to drive, right? Do you know how to get to Lake Pleasant?"

Phil nodded.

"Go there now, while it's dark. Throw the gun in the lake. Make sure no one sees you."

"But it's forty minutes from here. And I've never driven at night, or alone. And I don't even have a license—just a learner's permit."

The doctor said nothing.

"What if the police pull me over?" went on Phil.

"We'll worry about that if it happens," said the doctor. "Go. I'll stay here with your mother."

When Phil returned home at dawn, a police car was parked in the drive. Presumably, Dr. White had finally talked his mother into calling in a complaint.

Phil walked into the living room to see his mother crying hysterically while a policewoman attempted in vain to comfort her. Dr. White was arguing with a male officer, or rather trying to convince him of something while the officer listened on.

"Are you Phil?" asked the policewoman. "You may want to sit down here next to your mother."

Phil did so, listening to Dr. White going on about Mrs. Sumner's sleepwalking, which sometimes caused her to trip and fall on things. Tonight, she had fallen face first into the vanity in the master bedroom.

"Looks to me like she got beaten. Damn near bludgeoned to death," the male officer said.

"What it *looks like* is irrelevant. I'm her doctor, and I'm telling you what it *is*."

"I'm just saying—"

"We do not have time for this right now! Her diagnosis is on record in my files, which you can retrieve in the morning. Is this really what we should be talking about right now, minutes after you told us her husband's car had been flattened by an eighteen wheeler?"

Phil's mother wept at the funeral. He despised her for those tears. Whether they were affected or genuine, it made no difference to him. Either would have been too good for the son of a bitch, even if he did have to get scraped out of his expensive automobile.

She remarried some months later to Dr. White. A few years passed; Phil finished high school early and headed off to college. He visited his mother and stepfather occasionally, but every new piece of furniture in their new house, every new car in their garage, and every picture of White and his mother smiling on their tropical vacations seemed stained by his father's blood.

When his mother talked of his father, she did so as if his death had truly been a tragedy, and, moreover, a real accident. She must have known it had been suicide, he thought incredulously. Perhaps that was the reason why she kept mourning him on every anniversary of his death. She knew he couldn't shake the bonds of his alcoholism, so he went out on his own terms, out of a sense of duty to his family.

Well, good for you, old man, Phil thought. Even better for the rest of us.

The life insurance policy alone, never mind his inheritance, ensured that Phil would never want for much. He could go to medical school without having to take out loans. He could live the life of a wealthy doctor as soon as his formal medical education was finished, while most of his colleagues would struggle to keep their heads above water in the years following medical school and residency.

But the windfall did not make Phil either happy or grateful. Nothing his father's death gave him was worth his childhood. But there was a measure of forgiveness he could extend his father in death—a forgiveness that he found unable to extend his mother. Phil's anger toward her was like a cancerous cell, growing and multiplying unchecked as the years went on and contaminating all his adult relationships.

Whenever Phil made love to a woman, he secretly despised her for letting him take advantage, for letting him invade her body, for compromising her sense of propriety and decency because of a pathetic need for companionship.

In his professional life, no one seemed to take notice of his misogyny. After all, surgery had been a man's profession long before he arrived. There were particularly few female surgeons in his field, and he believed most of them didn't have the emotional detachment or pragmatic stamina needed for the work. Women were prone to letting their emotions overwhelm their reasoning, losing focus during crucial moments. They allowed their neocortex to become compromised, rendering them, however momentarily, useless during surgery, where a fraction of an inch or a second meant the difference between life and death.

The evening before his early morning flight to Europe, Phil finished smoothing out the clothes in his suitcase with deliberation, then walked into the den where Marisa had her easel set up. She was consumed with her work, finishing a painting she had been working on all day. Phil stood watching her for a while, then turned on his heel and was about to walk back out when he looked down and saw the tiny black drop of paint on the rug.

"Look at this! Did you see this?" Dr. Sumner said, pointing and turning toward his wife.

All he wanted was to end the evening with a nice single malt and a smoke on the veranda. He wanted quiet. He wanted to clear his mind before his big speech tomorrow. But now everything was ruined.

"Why do I pay for that studio of yours—pay for you to have a space for your little hobby—when I have to come home to find paint on my favorite rug?"

"I didn't realize I had spilled anything," said Marisa. "I'm sorry. The natural light from the windows is good in here, and I'm working on a still life. By the way, painting is not my hobby. It's my profession, and it's my passion."

"Profession my ass! You couldn't live off of what you sell—and you mostly sell to my friends and acquaintances. And when I met you, you had just dropped out of art school. How's that professional or passionate?"

Phil squatted to get a closer look at the rug.

"What, like you've never doubted yourself? Your direction? Your talents? Even in college?"

"Nope," he said without looking up.

"Well, I did, but I got over it. And I have the guts to admit it. And by the way, I don't need your friends to buy my paintings. I can sell my work on my own."

"Oh, really? Well, guess what, even if you found some dupes to buy your stuff, you wouldn't be able to live in a house like this on your own. You'd be living in your studio. In fact, how about you pack up your stuff and go stay there until I get back? Sleep on the fucking floor for a few days. Maybe then you'll appreciate what I've given you."

"Fine. Maybe I'll stay there longer than you think," Marisa said.

"Good. Go back to where I found you: broke and eating day-old scones at a café with all the rest of your bohemian-wannabe pals," said the doctor, touching the dried paint. The drop was solid and smooth under his fingertip.

"I may have been poor, but at least I was happy then," said Marisa, clenching her fist around her paintbrush and squinting at the canvas.

Phil didn't respond. His attention was entirely consumed by the black spot.

"Unsalvageable," the doctor said moments later, not noticing that his wife had thrown down her brush and left the room. He tried pulling the dried acrylic paint off, but it was deep within the weave. Only the size of a baby's fingerprint, it still ruined the rug.

# Chapter 7

## The Mausoleum — Houston, Texas

Pal leaned over the bar, rested his chin on his knuckles, and hummed loudly, trying to drown out a Depeche Mode bass line.

"You really don't care for this venture, do you, Palestrina?" asked Mistress Bovary, their Chosen One.

Pal did not want to talk to her, or to Gab, or to anyone. He just wanted to drink his draft beer in peace and try to ignore "Enjoy the Silence" blaring in his ears. But apparently, the Universe wanted him to entertain a dominatrix with civil discourse while his soon to be ex-friend was pop-locking in the middle of a huge, empty, strobe-lit dance floor.

"The S&M venture? Can't say that I am enthused, no," answered Pal. "Don't think my parents would be proud of me. I'm just humoring Gab."

"Is there really a need to be so insulting?" asked Mistress Bovary with more curiosity than rancor.

Pal scanned her getup once more. Red leather bustier. A devil tail swinging from her backside. Six-inch platform boots, also fire red. An oddly cute pair of horns. Pal wasn't sure if the tangles of blonde hair cascading down her back were natural or store bought. It was hard to tell without proper lighting. He thought a nice black flapper wig would have suited her much better.

She had almost given him a heart attack when she walked in looking like this. Apparently, she had come straight from a photo shoot, thinking that it wouldn't hurt to show her new partners what she was working with. Besides, she said, in the Mausoleum, no one was even going to look at her twice. She had been wrong. People had looked: twice, thrice, and more times besides. In the last twenty minutes, she had already sent back three drinks.

Pal regained his focus, blaming a few of the adult websites he frequented for overdeveloping his sensitivity to red leather and fishnets.

"I'm not insulting you or your chosen profession. Isn't it the oldest?" Pal said over the music. He thought he'd said something clever until he took his eyes off of Bovary's bosom and looked into her eyes.

"Do you have any idea what I actually do? Or don't do, for that matter? Let me clue you in: I'm not a prostitute, I don't have sex with my clients, and I'm not in this for the fast cash. And actually, I was a computer programmer before taking this up. But programming is a nine-to-five cubicle job. This line of work lets me set my own rate and my own hours, and frankly, the job security is better. And I'm not tied down to any place: I can take my show on the road, see the world, meet interesting people . . ."

"And spank them?" Pal interrupted. He had to. It was too easy. He only wished Gab was there to hear it.

". . . and help them deal with the day-to-day stresses of life. People need some form of release, emotional as well as physical, and I provide that for them."

Pal put his hand up.

"Okay, I get it," he said.

"How about we talk about you?" Bovary said.

"By all means," Pal said. "Tell me about me."

"I don't think you're just humoring Gab. I think you admire him."

"Admire him? Do you see what I see?" Pal said, pointing. Gab was doing "the robot" on the dance floor.

"God knows he looks up to you. You were all he talked about this afternoon, when he wasn't rambling about some married woman he's involved with. He has a lot of joie de vivre. You could use some of that yourself."

"Look, now he's doing 'the worm'!" Pal said.

"Are you always this removed?"

"Are you always this feisty?" He knew he was being rude, but he couldn't help it. The Mausoleum and its beer always did that to him.

"Okay," Bovary said, rising from her barstool. "Nice meeting you, Palestrina. Tell Gab thanks for the offer, but I'll find another studio."

"Wait, you're leaving? No demonstration of your . . . stress-relieving techniques?" Pal laughed. This wasn't real. His heart thing, now that was real. What did he care about this devil not in disguise?

Mistress Bovary smiled, gave Pal a couple of pats on the cheek, and exited the club with a gracefulness that made Pal's chest go all tight and tingly.

"Fuck," Pal gasped, pressing down on his sternum.

Gab must have seen her leave from the dance floor, because in the next seconds he was by the bar.

"Whoa, what just happened? Why did she leave?"

"She had to go," Pal answered, still looking at the door and hyperventilating a little.

"Did you piss her off? What did you say? You know, there's an intelligent, sensitive, and business-savvy woman underneath that tightly corseted leather exterior. Tell me you didn't piss off our meal ticket!"

"I only voiced some concerns about our foray into the fetish market."

Gab spun around clutching his fists, eyes rolled towards the heavens, or rather the roof of the old warehouse.

"Awwwwfuckmaaan!" he screamed, putting his hands in his sandy hair and pulling at it dramatically. "Why do you always have to voice concerns? If everyone went around voicing concerns all the time what kind of world would it be? Certainly wouldn't be the America we know and love, no sir! Just once, couldn't you keep your concerns to yourself?"

"I'll fix it," Pal said, somewhat ashamed now. He had only seen Gab this upset once or twice before. It was somewhat disconcerting. "Do you have her number?"

Gab gave Pal a strange, constipated look.

"Why? You don't think you've fucked up enough, and you want to finish a job well started?" Still, he pulled a business card out of his wallet.

Pal grabbed it out of his hand.

"Don't lose it. I don't have any more," Gab said.

Pal brought the card closer to the faux electric candle on the bar and read it aloud:

"'*Mistress Bovary – Sensualist – By Appointment Only.*' What the fuck kind of name is 'Mistress Bovary'? What's her real name?"

"I don't know," shrugged Gab. "I never asked."

Jessica had taken the name "Mistress Bovary" the night before she said goodbye to her mentor at Bush Intercontinental Airport.

She had fallen in with the fetish community after moving to Houston from Las Vegas the year before. She frequented the galas and balls thrown in secret dens by the upper echelon of the Bayou City. It was, on the whole, a welcoming and hospitable crowd. Everyone had alter egos to suit their fancies. She had been particularly amused by a regular who called himself Dog Boy, who was led around on a chain by a certain Miss Behave.

Although Jessica used her real name at such places, she did not ask for the names of her fellow fetish enthusiasts. They were all there to have fun, after all, not become bosom buddies.

She grew to love the sense of community, almost of family in this subculture. Men of means went around in ballroom gowns and high heels, looking prim and prissy as though they were at church. Women wrapped themselves in leather and ground against each other on the dance floor. Of course, the same people would never acknowledge each other if they chanced to meet in an antique store or the grocery store—that kind of camaraderie shunned daylight. But under the cover of darkness, their fellowship bloomed like a thousand perfumed flowers of delicious wickedness.

It was a veteran dominatrix that taught Jessica the ways of a domme. Her name was Mistress Shiva.

Shiva had taken a fancy to Jessica right away when she met her at a Christmas fetish ball, possibly because several others were already taking a fancy to her as well, and snatching her away from her grabby fans was an assertion of seniority.

"Were you at this event last year?" Shiva asked her, not bothering to introduce herself.

"No, I only moved here from Vegas in July," Jessica said.

"I didn't think so. I would have remembered you. This is the only one I still go to anymore. They are a bit too ostentatious for my tastes."

"Mine too, to be honest."

"I can show you a better side to this lifestyle, if you would care to leave with me."

"Now?"

"Now."

Jessica was not at all afraid. She knew this was not a pickup. She felt a maternal vibe from this older woman in latex. She sensed that whatever she had been unconsciously searching for might be revealed to her tonight.

Mistress Shiva took her by the hand and led her to her limo, where her driver smiled and opened the door for them. They drove to Shiva's private dungeon tucked away in the heart of Montrose.

"On nights like this, I leave my own car at home. It pays to keep up appearances. Besides, have you tried driving in nine-inch heels?"

At the dungeon, Shiva gave Jessica a tour of all the special rooms: the cage-cluttered Leopard Room; the Rubber Room, with chains hanging from floor to ceiling; the Suspension Room, with various sex swings; the Classroom, which had a chalkboard with the words "Professor Shiva — BDSM 101" written in elegant cursive.

The Medical Room was the latest addition, and the one Shiva seemed to be the most proud of. Jessica took a seat in an old dentist's chair and sipped her wine while Shiva reclined on an examination table and kicked off her immense heels with a satisfied groan.

"Do you have sex in this chair?" Jessica asked.

Shiva took a long, seductive drag of her cigarette.

"My dear child, a professional mistress does not have sex with her clients, do drugs with them, or engage in blood sport with them. No piercing, no cutting, no branding. Too unsanitary."

Jessica took another sip of wine.

"Here is what I do—and do damn well, I might add: spanking, flogging, caning, hair pulling, face slapping, immobilizing using leather arm restraints or Japanese rope bondage techniques. Those are fun. I did a seminar in Tokyo a while ago to learn them—not a cheap seminar, I must admit, but it paid off tenfold in recent years. Let's see, what else . . . nipple torture, up to a point . . . electrical play, also with some limiting factors . . . hot wax . . . trampling people underfoot with stiletto heels—and it takes some skill to do that right, believe me. And of course, the stage setting: forcing clients to lick my boots, gagging them with stockings, etcetera, etcetera, etcetera. Am I boring you?"

"Not at all. How did you get into this?"

"Let's leave that story for another day. I will say though that I have been doing this for a long, long time. How old do you think I am?"

"I dunno . . . thirty-five?"

Jessica was trying to be nice. Actually, Shiva looked to be in her forties, but they were well-kept and athletic forties.

"What would you say if I told you I was fifty-four? It's true. I look damn good for fifty-four, don't I? I tell you, this job is a great stress reliever. But all good things eventually run their course. I want to see the world beyond this dungeon."

"That's wonderful, Mistress Shiva," Jessica said. She still couldn't believe the svelte woman reclining across from her was in her fifties.

"There's another thing I've always wanted to do," went on Shiva. "Call it the romantic in me, but I've always wanted to take on an apprentice, teach a young girl like you everything I know. I want to give away all of my secrets before I move on. My peers are all as old as me, and besides, they won't appreciate my techniques. They would change them, switch the order of things, twist them to suit their own styles. Pervert them, as it were."

Shiva extinguished her cigarette and looked Jessica directly in the eye.

"So. Are you interested?"

The next months went by quickly. When she had no clients, Shiva showed Jessica how to communicate with subs, how to administer discipline, how to do basic rope work. Sometimes she brought in a friend to stand in as a sub, or have Jessica act the sub herself, to learn what things felt like on that end. She began to observe Shiva's sessions and eventually participate in them. Eventually, she became very adept at delivering exactly what the submissive wanted—even things they never asked for directly. Within a few weeks Shiva knew that her decision to pass the whip to Jessica, however impulsively she might have made it, had been the right call.

"Well, Honey Baby, I'll be leaving soon," Shiva said one afternoon after Jessica completed a session. "I've given you everything you need to make a solid start. I'll even throw a few referrals your way. I think you'll do just fine. Word about you is already getting around."

"Do your clients know that you're leaving?"

"I suppose. I haven't formally announced my intentions yet, but like I said, people talk. I'm sure some will be heartbroken, and many will refuse to come near you, my beautiful protégée. It's a form of loyalty. When someone you love breaks up with you, it's not exactly *comme il faut* to start dating his younger, cuter brother, is it?"

"What if I'm no good at this?" Jessica asked as she fidgeted with her new whip.

"I've seen you work. I wouldn't worry. You have excellent control."

"No, I mean, what if I'm no good at the business side of this?"

"My advice? Start small. Use a spare room in your apartment. Get comfortable with yourself and your clients. Eventually, you'll grow, the business will grow, and you can move it to a new place, a neutral place where you can separate work from play. If all goes well, in time you can scale it up to earn as much as you want, on your own terms."

"And what about my needs? Where does love fit into this equation?"

Shiva sat down on top of the teacher's desk in the Classroom and motioned for Jessica to take a seat across from her. The setting seemed appropriate: they were just coming out of a session where Jessica had ended up in a Catholic schoolgirl outfit.

"My dear, if you fall in love with the right person, one who understands . . . this." Shiva looked around the room, taking it in, as if trying to really see it for the first time. "If they understand this, you'll be just fine."

"And if they don't?"

"Well, if you fall in love with the wrong person, you'll lose the business, and eventually, you'll lose them as well."

"How do I know if I'm with the wrong person?"

"Funny how that works. If you're with someone who is horrible for you, it can take a while to recognize it. A long, long while sometimes. Doesn't matter how smart you are. The heart overpowers the head."

Jessica nodded.

"But when the right person comes along, that will be different. You will know it immediately. Heart *and* head."

"How do you know all of this?"

Shiva did not answer. Instead she hopped down from the desk, walked over to Jessica, and kissed the top of her head.

"I leave in a few weeks. Let's start getting things together," she said.

A few weeks later, Jessica said goodbye to her mentor at the airport.

Although Shiva offered to give Jessica her client list—a severe breach in dominatrix protocol—Jessica refused. She told Shiva she wanted to strike out on her own.

"Well, have you come up with a name for yourself? That's the first step."

"I'll tell you if you tell me your real name," Jessica said.

"My real name is Sheila. Pretty close to Shiva, right? It was the first thing I thought of all those years ago. Okay, your turn."

"Mistress Bovary."

Shiva shook her head in disapproval.

"That will never, ever work."

She kissed Jessica on the cheek and, after a long embrace at the passenger drop-off, was on her way to Barcelona. Jessica returned to her apartment in midtown Houston and started to hang chains from the ceiling in the spare bedroom.

# Chapter 8

Marisa's Studio — The Heights, Houston, Texas

The neighborhood where Marisa's studio was located reminded Gab of Deepwater: mom-and-pop bodegas littered with tempura-painted advertisements in Spanish, dozens of taquerias stretching down the avenues, countless mechanics' garages, liquor stores, and pawn shops.

Marisa's studio was within throwing distance of where she grew up and where her mother still lived. When she was a girl, a lot of white people lived here. She and her father, mother, and brothers and sisters had been one of the first Mexican families to move into the neighborhood. Now it was almost entirely Hispanic. Over the years, the boutiques and specialty stores closed, and new businesses took over: nail salons, Mexican restaurants, and dollar stores crept in and rooted themselves down in the district known as The Heights.

Gab tried to comfort Marisa as she sobbed on an old sofa in the studio.

"Marisa . . . Marisa . . ." he cooed softly, stroking her hair. Only minutes before they had been laughing, eating cold pizza for breakfast and watching *Roadhouse* on an ancient 10-inch TV.

"Sorry . . . I don't mean to involve you in my problems," Marisa said, wiping away the few tears Gab didn't get.

"I am involved," he said.

"There's a lot you don't know. I don't tell you everything. When you're around, I just want to have a good time. But I know you want more. It's wrong of me to keep stringing you along. If I were in your position, I'd be going crazy."

"I'm patient. I'll wait for you. A hundred years for one day. And if we end up only friends, that's fine, too."

"Gab, stop it. That's a lie. You're not being truthful with yourself or with me. I shouldn't have asked you to come here."

"I'm glad you did. Look, just talk to me . . ."

So she did. After all, who else was there?

"He says that I'm not a real artist. He says that my work sells only because of his influence," Marisa said, trying to soften her husband's remarks. "Why am I still with him?"

Gab didn't have a good answer.

"Because he's your husband, and you love him?" he said uncertainly.

"But I love you, too," said Marisa.

"I know," said Gab.

"God, I'm such a bad person."

Gab didn't like when things turned this emotionally awkward. When things got this deep, he lost all control of the conversation, especially when his feelings were involved.

Still, he tried.

"You just need to reinvent yourself!" he exclaimed. "Take that painting right over there, the one of the orchid. Do you like that painting?"

Marisa shook her head. "No. One of Phil's colleagues wanted a picture of an orchid for his dining room."

"To match his drapes?"

"Something like that."

Gab jumped up from the sofa and thrust his index finger toward the ceiling.

"To which I say, and to which you should definitely say: fuck the drapes!"

He strode over to the easel, took a paintbrush from the table beside it, dipped it into the small bowl of red paint, and splattered crimson across the canvas.

"Gab, no!" Marisa screamed, running across the room and grabbing the brush from him. "What are you doing? Do you know how long I've been working on this?"

"Come on! Do it! You know you want to! You hate this picture!" Gab screamed back.

"No!" Marisa screamed, louder, and threw the brush at him. It hit him square on the nose and left nearly half of his face red.

"You know I'm right!" Gab picked the brush up off the floor and dipped it into the bowl again as Marisa searched for a rag to wipe the red off the white canvas before it dried. Grabbing her by the arm, he spun her back around toward the orchid and tried to put the paintbrush in her hand.

"Do it! Violate this sad pseudo-Georgia-O'Keefe shit. Channel some Jackson Pollock, baby!"

"Gab!"

"Come on! Do it! You hate this picture! You hate everything about it!"

As he yelled, Marisa looked at the meekly geometrical *Phalaenopsis lindenii* on the canvas. She remembered researching it before painting it, buying several plants in various stages of bloom, photographing them from various angles. It was going to pay for her next set of brushes, acrylics, a new easel . . .

She looked at the brush in her hand, raised it, and flicked it over the canvas. A comet's tail of red clouded one of the flowers.

Marisa gasped, astonished at herself. Even though Gab had already ruined the work seconds earlier, she felt like she was standing over the painting with a bloodied knife.

Gab put his thumb to his chin with a curled index finger touching his bottom lip.

"Yes, yes, I like it. It's graceful, yet powerful: feminine, yet assertive. I'll take two: one for my dining room and one for the outhouse."

Marisa flicked the brush in Gab's direction. Then again, and again, until he grabbed her and pulled her to the ground. Gab had no idea where she learned how to wrestle, but soon Marisa was on top of him, pinning his arms down with her knees. For a moment he thought of sticking his tongue out toward her crotch but then thought better of it. There was no telling what she might do with that tongue if she caught it.

"Missed a spot," he said.

Marisa leaned down and kissed him, letting his arms go free. He placed his hands between her shoulder blades, but she pulled back.

"Sorry, I got caught up in the moment," she said.

"Okay," he said, pulling her in closer for their lips to meet again.

# Chapter 9

Bovary's Apartment — Midtown, Houston, Texas

The mid-October morning was humid. Pal felt perspiration start to dampen the shirt underneath his linen sport coat as he walked down West Alabama toward Mistress Bovary's apartment. Finding a parking spot near the apartments, condos, and town homes so early in the morning was next to impossible, so Pal had to park half a mile away.

He didn't admit to himself why he had dressed up a bit more than usual, rationalizing that it was only because he wanted to make a good second impression, having botched the first.

Finally, he found the right building and rode the elevator up to her floor. He had patted the sweat off of his forehead in the lobby restroom, but he felt beads starting to resurface despite the air-conditioned hallway. He checked her card again to make sure he had the correct apartment number and rang the bell.

A young woman answered the door. She was dressed in cloud print silk pajamas and wore thick-rimmed glasses. Her auburn red hair was pulled back in a ponytail.

"Oh, I'm sorry," he said, perplexed. "I must have the wrong place."

"Come in, Palestrina," Bovary smiled. "You can't wake me up this early and start ribbing me the moment you get here. Let me get some coffee in me first."

"Bovary?" Pal goggled.

"What, do you think I sleep in that devil costume or something?"

"Uhm," Pal managed. He had lost all of the words he had rehearsed. He had wanted his apology to be quick and painless, but now that he was here, he had a feeling that he had another thing coming.

She looked at him, patiently waiting for him to say something else. A strand of her dark red hair was hanging down her face. One of the lenses of her glasses was scratched. She looked . . . familiar but in a strange way. Like someone he should have met a long time ago.

"You look . . . normal," said Pal, immediately cringing on the inside.

"Is that your attempt at a compliment?"

"Sorry, I'm not good with words right now. You were right, it's too early."

"Come in, come in."

Pal looked around as Bovary closed the door behind him. The apartment décor was unexpectedly sedate. He had expected something darker, more ominous. Instead there were photographs of Tibetan monasteries and Buddhist monks in saffron robes hanging on the walls. A few faded prayer flags fluttered on the balcony railing. Pal took a few steps and almost knocked a potted Jade tree off an end table, catching it before it fell to the floor. Bovary smiled as she watched him.

"Nice place," he said. "Very, um, monastic. Peaceful."

"You should see the other room. Would you like some coffee?"

"Sure. Black, please," said Pal. He made his way to the couch. "Did you decorate the place yourself?"

"No, a normal nonperverted human helped me out. Although he was gay. Do you have a problem with gay men, too, Palestrina? Or just hookers like myself?"

Pal groaned under his breath as he watched Bovary pour the coffee. She was clearly enjoying herself a little too much.

"Come on, cut me some slack. Do you know how much effort it took for me to pull my head out of the ground and come here? I'm sorry about what I said. I don't know what came over me—besides the massive amounts of beer, I mean. I think I'm just angry at the world lately."

"Fair enough," she said. "Here's to getting off on a better foot."

"Yes. Cheers," Pal said and touched her coffee cup with his.

The coffee was nice. Pal thought it tasted Ethiopian, probably a blend from Whole Foods. He fancied himself something of a coffee aficionado, even though most of the coffee he brewed on daily basis came preground from a can.

"Before you put your head back in the ground, I have to ask you something," Bovary said. "How does one come to have a name like 'Palestrina'?"

"Oh, lord. It's a long story," Pal said. He used to love telling it when he was younger, often explaining his name even when no one asked. As he got older, he started to feel his audience's indifference, even after he worked on his delivery and cadence. When a girl on a first date with him yawned in the middle of the story, he decided to hang it up for awhile and hadn't trotted it out since.

"Come on, I'm all ears. Tell me. I promise not to pick on you like those other kids."

"Really?"

"Yes. It'd be too easy, anyway. You're not much of a challenge."

"Okay," Pal said. He pinched the bridge of his nose, trying to figure out the best way to begin. "Before I was born, my parents were happily married. Most of that happiness was due to the fact that they were married with no children. They had intended to keep it that way, but then my mother found out she was pregnant with me. She was distraught, because she felt that a baby would mean the end of the happy, almost carefree life she and my father had been enjoying up until that point. I mean, it was the swinging seventies. Not to say my parents were swingers or anything . . ."

"What, something wrong with that, too?" Bovary asked.

Pal's eyes widened.

"I'm kidding, I'm kidding. See? Too easy."

Pal smiled.

"She confided her fears to my father. He was a music teacher, and to cheer her up, he told her the story of Giovanni Palestrina."

"I'm starting to like this," Bovary said, taking another sip of her coffee.

Pal relaxed a bit. She did not look like she was going to yawn.

"Palestrina was a composer who convinced Pope Marcellus to allow for the composition of Church music that contained harmonies. The Pope had wanted complex music banned, because of satanic influences or something like that. Anyway, Palestrina said something like: 'Hey, let me just compose one thing for you with harmonies. Once you hear it, you'll love it, and it will change your whole perspective.' So he wrote some beautiful choral compositions with these harmonies and layers. The Pope loved them and said: 'Man! What was I thinking? This isn't satanic; it's great!'"

"And your father told your mother that story because . . . ?"

Mistress Bovary looked like she was trying hard to remember every detail of the story for future reference. Pal wondered if she was usually this attentive.

"Well, he thought of the new baby, me, as adding harmony to the already beautiful life he and my mother made together. He told her that things wouldn't get more complex or convoluted, just better on many levels."

"How sweet. So you are just one harmonious guy, a complement to everyone's melody, right?"

"Something to strive for, anyway," Pal said evasively.

He never told anyone the rest of the story. Shortly after giving birth to him, his mother disappeared, only resurfacing the day he finished kindergarten, right at his school. She told him she made a mistake by leaving, and that she loved him very much, but she had to leave again. Pal had no idea who this crazy lady was and told his father about her on the way to Showbiz Pizza, where they were heading to celebrate Pal's first graduation. His father opened his mouth, let out a faint gasp, and began to sob. He was still crying as they pulled into the parking lot.

Pal held his father's hand in the car until the tears stopped. Once inside the pizza place, Pal checked on him repeatedly until it was time to leave.

"Do you really think I'm a whore?" Bovary asked, interrupting Pal's time travel to 1978.

"What?" He shook his head. "No! Where did that come from?"

"I just want you to be honest, that's all."

"Look, I don't know you. I honestly don't know what to think about you."

"What do you feel?"

"I don't know what I feel."

Bovary's consternation showed on her face. Pal didn't like it. What did she want from him?

He started to fidget. Clearly, the world had not lied to him: all women were crazy—even the obviously crazy ones, with bullwhips hanging in their closets.

"What do you *want* to feel?"

Was that a *purr*? thought Pal in a near panic.

"Nothing . . ."

"Do I make you nervous? Even looking normal like this?" Bovary put her hands up to make imaginary quotation marks when she said the word "normal." Pal hated when people did that.

"It's not you," he said. He wanted to do his own little quotation gesture when he said "you," but he wasn't sure why. "Maybe it's your . . . Are you always so . . . ? I don't know. Women don't usually . . . uhm . . ."

"Don't usually what? Speak their minds? Voice their desires?"

"I don't know. Whatever you're doing. I didn't expect this."

Pal stood up to leave.

"Please, Palestrina, sit back down. The dungeon is in the next room. Here, come sit on the loveseat," Bovary said, patting the cushion next to her. "I'll keep you safe from the whips and chains . . ."

"It's not even that," Pal said. "Fuck! What am I still doing here? I have to go."

Pal made his way to the door. He realized he still held her business card in his hand. He looked at it and turned toward her. "Again, sorry about all the . . . that. Goodbye, Mistress Bovary."

"Please, my name is—" she said, standing up.

"I don't want to know," he interrupted. "I gotta go."

After Pal closed the door behind him, Bovary sat back down, shook her head, and grinned into her half-empty cup of cool coffee.

# Chapter 10

Marisa's Studio — The Heights, Houston, Texas

"I still can't believe we're doing this," Pal said as he and Gab prepared half of Marisa's studio for its transformation into a dominatrix lair.

"Well, let me tell you, we almost didn't, 'cause you almost blew the whole operation!" Gab said. "Twice! I had to beg and plead with Bovary. Now guess what? The new cut is eighty-twenty."

"Eighty-twenty?" Pal asked, flabbergasted.

"Yes, and I had to promise that you won't hang around here."

"Eighty-twenty?!"

"She thinks you need therapy. Not this kind of therapy, with whips and shit. I'm talking real therapy, brother."

"She really said that?" Pal asked, deflated. Then he noticed he was letting his hurt show and quickly regained his composure. "Whatever. What does she know? Even *you* think this idea is bullshit. Real therapy, huh?"

"That's what the woman said. Help me with this." Gab tried to lift something that resembled a nineteenth-century electric chair, except it had a huge codpiece attached to the front of the seat, where most of the voltage would no doubt be directed.

"What is *this*?" Pal asked, looking at the freakish piece of furniture.

"I think this is for the balls," Gab said, patting the metal codpiece. "Jesus Christ on a cross!"

"Don't criticize, Pal. This contraption has nothing to do with you. It's just a small part of a lucrative venture that will be beneficial to everyone involved."

Pal frowned and shook his head. Gab quickly switched gears.

"So, what exactly did you say to her?" he asked. "I mean, I thought she was pretty demanding before, but she really turned it up a few notches when I talked to her."

"I didn't say anything. I think she might have wanted to get, I don't know, intimate or something."

"Did she break out the whips and shit?"

"Will you please stop saying 'whips and shit'? Is that your new catch phrase? Or better yet, the name you're planning to give this clandestine crypt? Because it doesn't sound even remotely—"

Pal cut his rant short as Bovary entered the loft and began looking through boxes, picking up things from them, examining them, and placing them back.

"No, I did not break out the whips and shit," she said, not looking at either Pal or Gab. "And don't flatter yourself, Palestrina. I was just trying to get to know my new business partner," she said, still examining her gear. Today she wore thigh-high leather boots.

"Do me a favor. Get to know Gab instead."

Pal dropped the box he had been carrying as he stared at Bovary. She didn't look up at him.

Gab stopped trying to move the chair and mouthed "what the fuck?" to Pal.

"As a matter of fact, I have already gotten to know Gab somewhat. He was very receptive to my . . . technique," Bovary said.

"Really?" Pal asked Gab. "*Really?*"

Gab shrugged.

"I wanted a demonstration," he explained. "I had to test the services we were signing up to provide. It was strictly business."

"At first," Bovary said.

"Oh, I immediately knew we were on to something," Gab said. "The gag was totally unnecessary, though."

"You wanted a full demo."

"Oh, Lord," Pal groaned. "I really think I'm going to be sick. I need to leave."

"Some people just don't have the heart for this business, I guess," sighed Mistress Bovary.

Pal uttered something under his breath as he walked past her and out of the studio.

"Whoa," she said after hearing the entry door close. "What's his deal? That's the second time he has walked out on me."

"I think the heart comment might have got to him. Not your fault. I never told you."

"Never told me what?"

Gab positioned himself in the chair, careful not to get his testicles near their intended spot.

"He's scheduled for a heart procedure soon, so he's nervous about it, naturally."

"I was just speaking metaphorically," Bovary said. "How was I to know? It's not like it's apparent he's a heart patient. How serious is it?"

"Pretty serious. Some birth defect that has gone undetected all this time. Explains why he never was much for P.E. class or *Friday the 13th* movies."

Gab reached down and grabbed a riding whip and some sort of pointy-spiky-rubbery device from the box Pal dropped.

"How do you sterilize these things?" he asked the mistress. "*Do you* . . . sterilize?"

Bovary didn't respond, and Gab slowly put down the whip, dropped the other sex toy, and wiped his hands on his jeans. But the mistress was not paying his antics any attention.

"I've been kind of a bitch to him, even after he apologized. Payback, I guess. Trying to piss him off and then flirting with him, to get him all riled up and confused . . . You know, I might have a little crush on your boy. He's very cute when he's all flustered."

"Isn't being a bitch precisely what you get paid the big bucks for?" Gab asked.

"Not exactly," she said. "Not like that. I'm much more straightforward with my submissives. In my defense, he did call me a prostitute that night at that weird club. I just wanted to prove to him that I was legitimate."

"Well, you didn't need to prove your legitimacy to me."

"Come on, Gab. You were on all fours before I finished introducing myself. Palestrina's so different, so much more complicated . . . He did open up a little when he came to my apartment. Told me the story about how he got his name. It was like he was trying to reveal his true self to me. I'm a sucker for men who can let their guard down and expose themselves."

Gab snickered.

"Oh, grow up," Bovary huffed.

"Did he tell you about his ex-fiancée?"

"No. He didn't say much beyond the name story. I started ribbing him, and he ran out."

"A year ago, he proposed to his long-time girlfriend," Gab continued. "She said yes, then called it off out of nowhere and ceased to acknowledge his existence. So now he's a bit gun-shy with girls. But I can tell he liked you immediately."

"Well, if he did, he could have fooled me."

"You just have to know how to read him," Gab said. "Since his 'disengagement,' he's really been questioning things. And now this operation . . . Think of it as a pre-midlife crisis."

"Please," Bovary said. "Men go through a midlife crisis whenever a girl flirts with them in a bar. If there is one thing I understand, it's a man and his midlife crisis. Men love possibilities more than love. How do you think I get most of my clientele? It's when the success, the money, the power, and the stable, boring marriage don't add up to happiness. That's when they come see Mistress B. But you think I'm full of shit, don't you?"

"No, I think you're right on target."

"Really?"

"Yes ma'am. It's all about the thrill of the hunt. Once we capture our gazelle, sink our teeth into it, and feel its pulse slowly fade, we don't even bother to eat it."

"That's . . . very compelling imagery."

"Yeah, and from a vegetarian, no less."

Marisa entered the studio and looked around, holding a cupped hand to her mouth and trying not to giggle. The idea of sharing her space with an S&M lair was decadent and delicious. If only her husband could see her and her "bohemian-wannabe" friends now! The only time he had set foot into that studio was when the realtor was walking them through it.

"This is coming along nicely, guys," Marisa said.

"Marisa, have you met Mistress Bovary? She's the brains and brawn behind this whole venture."

"No, we've not been introduced. Gab speaks highly of you, Marisa," Bovary said, smiling graciously.

"You must have something pretty serious on him."

"The only thing is, I was under the impression the studio belonged solely to him. I hope we won't be too crowded in here," Bovary said, looking worriedly over the equipment still piled haphazardly on the floor. "Hey, can we put the whipping rack over in this corner?"

"Yeah, right there looks really nice," Marisa said, trying to help.

"We will have to put up some dark drapes to divide to room. You don't mind, do you?"

"No, not at all. I have a couple of folding screens around here somewhere that we can use in the meantime. As long as I get all the windows and you get all the dark corners, it all works out. I'd love to help you decorate."

"Thank you so much."

"Don't mention it."

"Gab raves about your paintings. I can see why," Bovary said.

"Oh, it's all crap, really. There was a time when I tried to be cutting-edge."

"Hey, you're still cutting-edge," Gab interrupted. "What about that last piece—the one I inspired?"

"The blood-splattered orchid? Inspired my ass . . ."

Gab put a finger to his lips and frowned, as if in deep thought. "'The Blood-Splattered Orchid Inspired My Ass.' Definitely has a ring to it. Now, is that just a working title, or . . . ?"

"Okay, now I have to see it," said Bovary.

"Come on." Marisa gave Gab a half-hearted glare. "I'll show you *my* half of the studio."

Walking away, the women did not notice Gab climb onto a torture rack, where he would eventually get stuck.

# Chapter 11

Café Comitatus — River Oaks, Houston, Texas

Noisy and crowded as it was, Café Comitatus was still the only place Pal could get some peace. Perhaps it was precisely the crowd that did it: the more people at the counter and the tables, the more alone Pal felt. And there was always a crowd. The German chocolate cake was overpriced and not as good as, say, the frozen Sarah Lee brand from the grocery store, but the River Oaks people ate the shit out of it.

Pal drank his coffee in the darkest corner of the café. When he got up for a refill, he saw his ex-fiancée sitting alone near the cake display case.

"Fuck," Pal muttered, wondering how he was going to sneak back to his own table without being seen.

"Pally?"

Pal hated this nickname. Even when she used it affectionately, it still came out demeaning. Also, it made his ex sound vaguely like Charles Bronson.

"Palestrina's fine," he said.

"Yeesh, sorry," she chuckled. "Wanna sit with me?"

Pal didn't, but it was not his nature to be rude, even to the person who ripped out his heart and stomped on it publicly in a furniture store.

He regretted his decision immediately.

"So, how have you been?" he forced himself to say.

"Good. How about yourself? Seeing anyone new yet?"

She was as direct and forthright as he remembered. It used to turn him on; now it just made him nauseous.

"Is that really an appropriate question, considering?" he said. "What gives you the right to pry into my life?"

"Oh, here we go," she said. "Listen, Pally, I just wasn't ready. You're a practical guy, you understand. I'm practical, too. When you whipped that ring out, you totally caught me off guard. I said yes because I figured it'd buy me some time to think. And when I thought about it, I realized we weren't ready. I wasn't ready. I wanted to explore my other options. Why did you have to rush things like that? It's not like I'd have never married you. Maybe I would have, eventually." She shrugged. "We were quite good together."

When she was fifteen, Pal's ex—he refused to refer to her by name anymore, even inside his own head—had read *The Fountainhead*. As a result she became obsessed with the idea of marrying an architect or some other industrially creative type dripping with integrity. She couldn't imagine anything more romantic than a man building something from the ground up despite insurmountable odds. That's what she said, anyway. But Pal saw something else she took away from Ayn Rand, something dangerous to any man, woman, or pack of wolves: deep within her subconscious, she had learned to worship egotism and loathe altruism, even in the form of basic human decency.

"You could have told me you needed more time," Pal said. "You didn't have to pretend to go along with it and then suddenly break things off, just because that was more convenient."

"What can I say, I got caught up in the moment. And then afterwards, I just couldn't bring myself to do it. You looked so happy. But after a while, I realized I couldn't keep it up any longer."

"You left me with the rent. Remember your expensive apartment downtown? The one you couldn't afford on your own, so I moved in?" Pal thought of his condition and tried to calm down. It would not do for his last earthly image to be the bitch sitting across from him. "Ah . . . forget it. Water under the bridge. How is life?" he said, trying to smile.

"Well . . ." She paused, trying to suppress a smile. "God, I don't know how to say this . . ."

"Say what?"

She didn't end up having to say anything. A tall, handsome blond approached the table. He was holding an engagement ring between his thumb and forefinger.

"Hey, baby," he said, coming up from behind and thrusting the ring before her eyes. "Guess what got in today from New York City?"

He slid the ring onto her finger, and Pal saw a huge solitaire reflect in her eyes—again.

"Oh, baby, it's perfect," she said.

"Oh, God . . ." groaned Pal.

"Baby, this is Pally," said the ex. "I was just about to tell him about your proposal."

"Oh, darlin', you always bore your friends to death with that story."

The man extended his hand toward Pal.

"Pleased to meet you, Pally," he said with a sincere and pleasant smile. "Name's Buck Tadlock."

"Condolences on the engagement," Pal said, shaking his hand.

The smile wavered. "Excuse me?"

"Baby, I forgot to warn you," said the ex sourly. "Palestrina is the passive-aggressive sort."

"Wow, princess, way to go!" Pal said. "You finally got my name right after all these years!"

"Listen, friend. I think you'd best leave," Buck said, squeezing Pal's hand harder before letting it go. Pal put both hands up to signal he didn't want any trouble.

"I apologize. I haven't had a chance to drink my coffee yet," he said. "I'm no fun to be around when I'm undercaffeinated. Have you tried the house blend here? Here, allow me."

Only as Pal watched his coffee flow down the handsome blond man's head, camel's hair jacket, and faded blue jeans, did he finally put two and two together: this was the boxer his fiancée had left him for.

He was already stumbling backwards when the blow came.

# Chapter 12

Marisa's Studio — The Heights, Houston, Texas

Eventually, the girls freed Gab from his predicament on the bondage rack after hearing his cries for help. Marisa was tempted to use the cat-o'-nine-tails after convincing Bovary to expose his ass, but the thought was fleeting.

"Hey! Pull my pants back up! Pantsing at the workplace is sexual harassment!"

"How do you get your ass to be so smooth?" asked Bovary, resisting the urge to palm. "Do you wax?"

"Once a year," said Gab as he got down. "What the hell were you guys doing over there so long? I was stuck for hours!"

"You were only up there ten minutes, at most."

Gab pulled up his boxer shorts and pants.

"I respect what you do, Bovary, but damn. Doesn't anyone get hurt when they are with you?"

"Only in good ways. That's what they pay me for. You're just a bit sensitive."

"Evidently . . ." Gab rubbed his wrists, which were raw from his attempts to free himself.

"Speaking of sensitive boys, you should check up on Pal. Maybe call him or something," suggested Bovary.

"Nah, he wouldn't answer his phone right now. Besides, I know where he is. This one upscale cafe in River Oaks. He always goes there when he wants to be alone and when he wants me to find him."

On his way to see Pal, Gab ran into an old friend who had been stationed in Germany for the past four years, so they detoured to see Gab's former applicant, Brandi, who was working the stage at Centerfolds Gentlemen's Club that night.

"I really like your work," Bovary told Marisa as they sat alone in the kitchenette over a bottle of cheap but decent red. Marisa was well stocked in that respect—since she left home, she had been averaging a bottle a night by herself, so she bought by the case.

"It's mostly sellout crap," Marisa said.

"Okay, fine," Bovary chuckled. "But the wine is fantastic. So light-bodied . . . cloves, summer berries . . . Where did you find it?"

"Big Daddy's Discount Cellar, across the street. Six ninety-five plus tax."

"I take back nothing," Bovary said. "It's still great. So, where is this new painting Gab said he inspired?"

"Oh, he's just talking. That boy lo-oves to talk. It's like he's emotionally invested in living up to his name for some reason."

"Don't I know it. He's like a fountain of randomness. Frankly, I don't think I have any business hearing half the stuff he says."

"Really?" Marisa asked. "What sort of stuff does he say?"

"Stuff about you and him, mostly."

"Oh, Jesus . . ." Marisa's head drooped.

Bovary grimaced.

"Shit. I'm sorry. I shouldn't have said anything."

"No, don't apologize. It's just . . . uncomfortable."

"Yeah."

"But it's over now. That's the important thing. And we stayed friends. We just got caught up in a moment a couple of times, and I let it go on too long."

"Hey, you don't have to explain. I'm not in the business of judging people. Kind of the opposite," Bovary said, nodding towards the dungeon behind the newly placed room dividers.

Marisa laughed.

"So, what about your non-sellout crap?" Bovary asked before Marisa stopped laughing. "Do you have any pieces for sale here? I've been wanting to invest in a breakout artist for a while."

"I have a few in storage. Tell you what: you open the next bottle, and I'll pull up a catalog for you." Marisa opened her laptop.

"Deal."

As Bovary uncorked the second bottle of Big Daddy's discount Grenache, her eyes fell on the colorful pictures stuck to the refrigerator with fruit magnets. One in particular caught her eye: Marisa with a man, clearly her husband, on their wedding day. Bovary set the bottle down and took the picture off of the door to examine the man closer.

"No . . ." she said.

|PART TWO| October 2002 – November 2002

# Chapter 13

Montrose Police Station – Houston, Texas

Pal and Buck sat cuffed to one another next to a desk in the police station. Pal had a split lip and a narrow gash above his eyebrow. Dried blood was smeared across his cheek from where he had wiped his nose. Thankfully, it was not broken, and neither was his jaw, though both pulsed with pain. Buck looked normal except for the coffee-stained jacket and messed-up hair.

"How about this," he said. "If neither of us ever sees you again, I won't press any charges."

"Fine by me," Pal said. He couldn't believe the idiot thought that he had actually been stalking that she-demon.

"You know something?" Buck said. "I never thought I'd actually meet you, much less whip your ass."

Buck was no stranger to fights, but this one left him uneasy. Usually, he tried to be a gentleman about it: with his 23-3-1 record with 14 knockouts, he had nothing to prove to anyone. When challenged, he usually took the guy outside, gave him a couple of jabs with his right, then threw a left cross no one ever saw coming, and it would be over.

However, Buck had never had someone pour scalding hot coffee over his head. This time, he had thrown his left immediately. And then . . . well. He was not proud of himself.

Pal said nothing.

Buck nudged him with his shoulder.

"Can you just leave me alone, please?"

Pal's head was splitting. He was sure more than one man had pummeled him after he fell to the ground. Maybe someone had accidentally stepped on his face. That had to be it.

"Hey, the least you can do is hear me out," Buck said. Pal heard a surprising hint of real anger in his voice.

"Why?"

"Because I've had to listen to stories about you for months now, for starters."

Pal shuffled in his seat. The handcuffs were killing him. Even worse, his ass was beginning to itch.

"She talks about me?" he said between wriggles.

"Yes, and I can't stand it. Each time I banged your head on the floor back at the coffee house, all I could think about was her singing your praises: what a great guy you were, what a generous lover you were. It drives me crazy!"

Pal decided to take pity on Buck. The guy seemed like a good sort, even if he did beat the crap out of him. If he could let him score a glimpse of the backstage machinery, at least the poor bastard would know what was turning the wheels behind the drama.

"She used to do that to me, too," Pal said.

"What?"

"Yeah. All the time, she'd go on about the guy before me. It's her way of keeping you close by undermining your confidence. I don't think her self-esteem is what she makes it out to be. I'm no one special. Think about it: if I were, she'd be wearing my engagement ring now, not yours."

"I'm pretty wealthy. Old money. I think that's maybe one of the reasons she sticks around."

"Nah," said Pal, feeling generous. "You must have something she really loves."

But that big-ass ring is a good start, he thought with a trace of bitterness.

"Thanks, buddy. You didn't have to say that," Buck said.

"Yeah, well, that's me. A real fucking Samaritan."

They had to sit for another hour before an officer came to the desk.

"You both just got lucky as shit. The owner of the cafe says he won't press any charges—if he never sees either one of you again. Got me? If you do go back there, I'll take pleasure in personally whooping your fairy asses myself."

"Didn't know this precinct was so attached to that coffee shop," Pal said. "But I guess they do have nice donuts."

"Watch your mouth, or I'll have you and your boyfriend in a cell faster than you can squeak and look the other way while he finishes giving you that makeover," the officer said.

"Actually, we've sorted out our differences, sir," Buck said lightly. "And may I add, on behalf of myself and my new friend, thank you for the opportunity."

He knew his lawyer would come through. Whatever the problem, dropping the Tadlock name usually did the trick.

"Can you take the cuffs off?" pleaded Pal, whose ass had fallen asleep.

"Oh, sure thing. Just gonna finish my chai mocha latte here." The officer laughed and licked a foam moustache off his upper lip. "Not bad. Never had one before. Next thing you know, I'll be voting Democrat."

Eventually, the cop's portly partner took pity on them. Both cops smiled and waved sarcastically at their captives as they watched them limp out of the station.

"Make a good couple, don't they?"

"Cute. Real cute."

# Chapter 14

Bovary's Apartment — Midtown, Houston, Texas

"Lick my boots."

"I don't like—"

Mistress Bovary yanked the chain attached to the client's dog collar.

"Did I say you could speak? Lick them!"

"Yes, Mistress!"

The half-naked balding man in lace-trimmed red panties hurriedly pressed his tongue to the bottom of Bovary's black knee-high boot.

The doorbell rang.

"Stay put, Harold," she commanded, wondering why her next client was an hour early.

"What do I do?"

"Um . . . drink from the doggy bowl," she said as she grabbed her robe and ran to the door.

It was Pal. His lip and right eye were swollen, and half of his face seemed to be caked with dried blood.

"Christ! Palestrina! What happened to your head?"

"I got into a fight. Are you busy?"

"I'm almost finished with—" She looked over at Harold, who to her surprise was actually lapping water enthusiastically from the dog bowl. "Never mind. Come in."

"Thanks," Pal said, flopping down on the couch, oblivious to the man on all fours drinking water from a dog bowl to his right.

"Let me get you something for that." Bovary rushed into the kitchen. "Sorry, Harold," she shouted to her client apologetically. "I'm going to have to cut our session short this evening."

"Of course, Mistress. May I get up?" Harold asked, somewhat peeved.

"Yes, Harold. Good boy."

Harold rose to a dignified bipedal stance.

"What happened to you?" he asked Pal as he took his clothes off a tall moveable clothes rack by the wall.

"I got into a fight," Pal answered, barely moving his tongue. The sight of a pudgy man with a dog collar rising out of nowhere almost ended his earthly existence.

"Looks like you lost."

"I lost a long time ago," sighed Pal.

"Do you have legal representation concerning this matter?" Harold asked. He had his shirt on and was now tying his soggy tie, which had apparently fallen off the rack into the dog bowl. The dog collar and chain flung behind his back made him look like the Road Warrior's accountant.

"Thanks, but I don't need a lawyer."

"No scamming my friends, Harold," said Bovary sternly. She had brought a bag of frozen peas from the kitchen.

"Guys, I'm all right," said Pal. "I don't need anyone's help, in either a Matlock or Dr. Quinn Medicine Woman sense."

"Here, take this just in case," said Harold, handing Pal a card. "I once represented a man who was assaulted upon entry into a place of business by an employee working late. I got a five-figure out-of-court settlement for him. Think about it."

Bovary rolled her eyes. "Harold, your client was robbing the place!"

"Not bad, right?" grinned Harold.

Pal remembered the case. It was all over the news a few years back. After breaking a lock and entering a store through the back door, the thief was met with a cattle prod to the testicles—repeatedly—until the police came. The criminal made a statement to the press saying he would never visit Boot Kicker's Western Wear again.

"He seemed nice enough," Pal said after Harold left.

"Here, let me help you." Bovary patted his eye with a wet washcloth and opened a first aid kit. Pal didn't say a word. It was an enormous kit; he supposed in her line of work, accidents did occasionally happen.

She cleaned his gashes with water, then with peroxide, then applied butterfly stitches. Pal never took his eyes off of her. Normally, that sort of thing would have creeped her out, but Pal's stare made her feel warm and achy inside.

"I want to take you out," Pal said finally. "Let's go somewhere."

"It's almost one o'clock in the morning. Where are we going to go?"

"I don't know. I don't care. I've been an asshole. I want to prove to you that I'm not really one."

"To me or to yourself?"

"Both, maybe. Please? Let's go get some coffee."

"Well, okay, but let me change. I can't be seen in public wearing my work clothes—again. Last time that happened, some guy with a funny Italian name came to my apartment the next morning, then ran off and came back the next night with the shit beat out of him."

# Chapter 15

"That's the last of it, I think. Look at this place, Marisa! It's so—"

Gab searched for the right words but came up bust. He had spent most of the night putting the final touches on Mistress Bovary's studio. Of course, she would have the last say, but the mood had struck him to be proactive. He had only the vaguest idea of what kind of decor the art of dominance called for, so he used his imagination.

"Fabulously creepy?" Marisa offered.

Gab turned toward her. Marisa was sitting on a brushed metal chair, and she looked gorgeous. "What do you think? Should we break the place in? We have a lovely assortment of leather whips, gags, and—whatever these are . . ."

"Don't come near me with any of that stuff," warned Marisa.

"Oh, I wasn't going to be the whipper—I was going to be the whippee," he said. "You know I could never hurt you."

Marisa opened her mouth to say something, but then closed it and looked away from him. She took a deep breath.

"What's wrong?"

"I'm pregnant, Gab," she said softly. "It might be yours."

Gab lowered the hand that was holding a whip.

"Did you hear me?" she almost whispered.

"Yes."

"Well?"

Gab looked down at his bare feet, then raised the whip again and pointed it at Marisa like an accusing finger.

"You have been a *ba-aad* girl," he said in an oddly flat voice, walking back over to the rack. "We're going to need a bigger whip."

"Gab, can you be serious for one minute?"

He stopped his posturing and looked at her, feeling like he was seeing a stranger.

"Are you sure?" he said quietly.

"I'm sure."

"I mean, are you sure it might be mine?"

Gab had no idea why he would say such a thing. It seemed like the appropriate comment to make for an adulterer.

"I mean, we use protection," he tried to elaborate.

"Not always. Not lately. Gab, what are we going to do?" she asked. "You know I can't . . . you know."

It didn't take long for Gab to make up his mind.

"Let's have it together! Give the old mean doctor the boot and come live with me. This is divine intervention, babe. This is a higher power saying, 'Look you two idiots, can't you see you belong together? No? How about now? Boom! Pregnant.'"

"It's not that easy."

"Why not? Tell him! Tell him the truth. Tell him you love me! Just leave him!"

"Leave him and go where? Come on, Gab! I'm a struggling artist. And you've not held down one steady full-time job since I've known you. You have no ambition."

"What do you call this?" Gab's voice went up an octave as he waved to the elegantly threatening devices all around him.

"I call this me humoring you. Do you really think this place will work out? You think you can live off your ten percent cut or something? Have you done any math on this at all? How do you expect to support m . . . a family?"

"Support you?"

Marisa ran her fingers through the hair at her temples.

"I didn't mean to say that. Of course I don't expect anyone to support me . . ."

"Sounded like a Freudian slip."

"Shut up!" she screamed, enraged. "Don't you fucking understand that if I leave him, then all my contacts, all of my buyers will be gone, too?!"

She shocked herself. I guess I do believe this, she thought, remembering Phil's accusation.

Gab looked at her with sadness.

"So find another job," he finally said. "Wait tables. *Teach* art."

"I don't want to teach art, or wait tables. I like my life the way it is."

"What life? Being kicked out of your own home by your rich jackass husband like a misbehaving dog?"

"I don't know what to tell you," Marisa said. "I'm trying to be honest."

"Tell me that you'll leave him, and that we'll raise the child together."

Marisa's eyes scanned the dungeon.

"I think I need some time to myself," she said. "I need to think."

# Chapter 16

Pie Hole — Upper Kirby, Houston, Texas

Pal and Mistress Bovary arrived at the Pie Hole before the two a.m. rush. To Pal, Bovary looked just as seductive in her sweatshirt and ripped blue jeans as she had in her sexy devil costume the first night they met. And Pal looked just as handsome to Bovary, even with his lip busted and one eye swollen half closed.

"Can I ask you something?" he asked as he stirred the coffee put in front of him by a drowsy waitress. "Were you going to have sex with that guy before I showed up?"

"I thought we went over this. I never have sex with my clients."

"Never?"

"Never. Not in any true sense of the word. My clientele is mostly new to the BDSM world. They come to me out of curiosity more often than of genuine desire. We keep it light, relatively speaking. If they want more than I am ready to provide, I refer them to someone else. Sometimes they come back to me. Quite often, actually. You never forget your first."

"Ever think about giving it up?"

"Nope," said Bovary, a bit too quickly. Pal didn't press the issue.

"So, what's the Palestrina story?" asked Bovary between sips of coffee. "And I'm not talking about the Renaissance composer. I'm talking about you."

"What do you want to know? There's not much to tell."

"Why do you keep knocking on my door?"

"I don't know. I really didn't mean to leave so suddenly last time. I'm just—ah . . . I can't explain it. I suck at analyzing my own feelings. And I have this thing with my heart . . ."

"I know. Gab told me. Had I known sooner, I wouldn't have . . . I don't know . . . toyed with you so much."

Pal shook his head.

"Don't worry about it. You did nothing wrong. I'm just very aware of my own mortality right now," he said.

"Are you afraid of dying?"

"Isn't everyone?"

"Sure."

"I guess I'm really more afraid of not having lived than of dying. I've always been afraid of that. When I met with the doctor, and he said I had this congenital heart defect, it all came to me. I've lived such a boring, vanilla life. You know: went to college, got a degree, got a job, got a girl, got marr—asked her to marry me."

"Oh?"

"She said no. Eventually. After screwing with my head for a while. Gave me some bullshit excuse of how she wanted to explore her options. Actually the option she ended up exploring was one of her crushes. Anyway, after she said no, everything just seemed to stop. I became kind of antisocial, lost touch with just about everyone. Except Gab. He refused to leave me alone. But that turned out for the best. I mean, I know he can be annoying as hell, but he always cheers me up, helps me to not feel sorry for myself."

Pal swirled the rest of his coffee in the cup. "Eventually I said, 'Okay, you're alone now. But it's not so bad. You like being alone.' That's what I told myself—that being alone was better than all the relationship drama. So I stopped looking. Or even really thinking about looking.

Until . . . I know it sounds corny, but then you came around." Pal sounded slightly embarrassed yet earnest.

"I understand," said Bovary, smiling slightly. "I'm weird, my job is provocative . . ."

"No. I mean, yes, it is—it's exciting—but that's not it."

"So what is it?"

"You're *real*."

"Oh?" Bovary said again, somewhat at a loss.

"I mean . . . I know we only met a few days ago, and I've only seen you for, like, a few hours total, but I still feel like I already know who you are."

"After a few chats where you did most of the talking? That's a bit presumptuous, don't you think? There are things about me—"

"I'm sorry. I didn't mean to sound condescending. I'm just rambling. I do that when I'm nervous. Ignore me."

"There's no reason to be nervous. And there's no need to convince yourself that you're falling for me just because you want to sleep with me. I understand physical attraction. I embrace it. It's not wrong. You don't have to butter me up with this you're-so-special, I've-never-met-anyone-like-you routine. I've never met anyone like you, either, but that doesn't mean I want to wed you. I wouldn't object, however, to going back to my place for what you really have in mind."

Pal sat motionless. Bovary touched his hand.

"Now, let's talk about your heart. Just how physical can you get?" she asked.

"I'm sure we can . . . uhm . . . work something out. I think if we—"

"Pay the bill, Palestrina."

# Chapter 17

Bovary's Apartment — Midtown, Houston, Texas

As she thought about waking Pal, Bovary heard a knock at the door. She put on her sweatshirt and went to answer. The super had probably received some more noise complaints last night. Ironically, this time the noise had not been made by a client.

She swung the door open. Her mouth fell open with it.

"Phil?" Bovary asked, shocked to see the doctor.

"Hey there, hot stuff," he said, coming in for a kiss that landed on her cheek when she abruptly turned her head to the side.

"What are you doing here?" she asked, her jaw clenched. Something was different in Phil's demeanor. He seemed loose and jittery, almost drunk, though he didn't smell of alcohol.

"I came to see my favorite mistress of the night!" the doctor said with a wide smile that showed too many teeth.

"It's eight in the morning, Phil. Shouldn't you be at home?"

"I just arrived. My plane landed an hour ago. I had to see you."

"Come back later, Phil," Bovary said.

Dr. Sumner frowned. Something was amiss. Bovary was never terribly thrilled to see him as of late, but she wasn't usually this standoffish.

"Why? You can't have a client this early." His eyes scanned the apartment.

"Go away, Phil."

"Wait. Is someone here?" Dr. Sumner asked, realizing he was about to get an answer he wouldn't like.

"You can call me in a few hours. Bye." Bovary tried to close the door.

"Just a minute. Who's here?"

Dr. Sumner pushed his way in and started toward the bedroom, shoving Bovary aside. She grabbed his bicep and struggled to pull him back towards the front door.

"No one," she said, trying to whisper and yell at the same time. "And I don't remember inviting you in."

Phil turned to her. His eyes gleamed with unhealthy excitement. "You know, I'm leaving my wife," he confided. "So you can quit all of this S&M stuff. You won't need it when you're with me."

"Are you out of your mind?"

"Is that any way to talk to your future husband?"

"I'm serious, Phil."

"Come on, Jessica. You're almost thirty years old. It's time to wise up. You can't keep messing around like this forever. What about when you have children? Are you going to let them play with your sex toys?" Dr. Sumner walked over to the window looking out to downtown Houston. The low sun shone brightly in the cloudless sky; he became a silhouette against the glass. "Hey, where are your widgets, anyway? Didn't that weird chair used to be right here?"

"There won't be any children," Bovary muttered. Somewhere in the back of her mind she knew this might not be the case, but she wasn't about to tell Phil.

"Sure there will. All women want children. You're lying to yourself if you think otherwise."

Pal awoke to the sound of Bovary talking to another man in hurried, clipped sentences. He was not even disappointed, he told himself. After a wonderful night like that, of course there would be some kind of a glitch in the morning. Just his usual luck manifesting itself.

He listened to Bovary argue with the vaguely familiar voice in his half slumber. Who could it be? he wondered. Gab, dropping in to tell her about yet another screw up? Didn't sound much like Gab though . . .

"Bov? Everything okay?" he called out from the bed.

Bovary popped her head into the bedroom. "Yep, everything's fine," she said, sounding and looking frazzled.

"So! No one's here, huh?" Dr. Sumner asked, leaning against the window and crossing his arms. He looked disappointed rather than jealous, like a parent busting a teenager mid-climb back into her bedroom window after a long night out.

Deciding to go see what the fuss was about, Pal leaned over the edge of the bed and began to scan the floor for any article of clothing that might be his.

"Phil, this doesn't concern you. I've asked you already—leave," Bovary said.

"I thought you didn't fuck your clients," Dr. Sumner said.

"He's not a client. He's someone I'm seeing."

"'Seeing'! Oh ho, that's rich! And you're going to tell me he's okay with what you do?"

"Get out!"

"Bov, what's going on?" Pal asked from the bedroom. He was still searching for any piece of lower-half clothing that would allow him to walk out of the room at least partially decent.

"I'll tell you what's going on, whoever you are!" Phil barked. His arms were still crossed, and he made no attempt to move. "You're not the only one she's fucking. And let me drop something else on you: you know how your girlfriend and I met a few years ago?"

"Phil, get out!" screamed Bovary.

Pal stopped looking for his clothes, partly to listen to the stranger's voice, and partly because he remembered that last night's interesting bits had begun in Bovary's kitchen, and all of his clothes now lay near the dishwasher.

"You girlfriend here was a whore! Top notch. Five-diamond level!"

"That's it, I'm calling the cops," said Bovary and began pressing phone buttons.

But Phil was already walking out of the apartment. At the door, he turned to look at her, but she slammed the door in his face.

When she turned back around, Pal was standing at the bedroom entrance wrapped in a sheet from the waist down. He had just missed the doctor.

Bovary closed the front door and leaned against it. Pal's face betrayed little, but she had a good idea of what thoughts must be racing through his mind.

"I'm sorry you had to hear that," she said. "I understand if you want to leave, but please, let me explain first . . ."

"I just need to . . . my clothes are in the kitchen."

Pal walked across the room. He did not want to look at Bovary, but she grabbed his shoulder as he bent to pick up his pants.

"Please. I need to tell you."

"Okay," Pal said evenly, looking into her eyes.

"Can we sit down?"

Bovary sat on her couch and turned her head away as Pal dressed. He finished putting on his pants and sat down in the chair opposite her.

She remained silent. Oppressed by the quiet, Pal became aware of the pain in his jaw, nose, and eyebrow. They throbbed rhythmically as if keeping time with a metronome. Concentrating on the pain calmed him a bit. Physical pain he could understand.

"The man who just left here wasn't lying, although he might have put it more delicately. I used to work as a call girl. He was one of my regular clients."

Pal grunted ever so slightly. If Bovary noticed, she made no sign.

"Eventually, he got attached to me and offered to get me out of that life," she continued. "I made good money, but I was not happy. I knew he was married when we started seeing one another, but he was . . . persistent, and generous, and I gave in. He found this place for me, helped me pay rent . . ."

"Are you still with him?"

"No, we split up. He didn't like my new line of work. And frankly, I didn't like him all that much."

Pal slipped on his shoes and rose from the chair.

"You seem to have liked his money well enough."

Bovary stood up and stepped toward Pal, who did not move.

"I understand you're upset. I'm not proud of that part of my life. That's why I took such offense to your comment about my current work. It hit a soft spot. It's not who I am anymore."

Pal could not look at her.

"Even if this thing between us was just going to be a one-night stand, you should have told me," he said. "I can't do this."

Pal inhaled sharply.

"I thought you were honest. *Real*."

"I *am*," she said. "It's been over between him and me for awhile. I have no idea what drove him to barge in here like this."

Pal said nothing but simply turned around and followed Dr. Sumner's steps out of the apartment and down the hall to the elevator.

# Chapter 18

Marisa's Studio – The Heights, Houston, Texas

Marisa sat on a couch, staring vacantly at the splotched orchid painting hanging crookedly on the wall when Gab rushed in. He had that wide-eyed look about him that told her he intended to disclose something he presumed to be spectacular.

"Guess what?" he said, not waiting for an answer. "So yesterday, after I left here, I needed a drink, see, and long story short, I walked out of McEwan's—wasn't that the place we met? With the drunk football players and the dartboard? Or were they soccer players? Anyway, I walked out, mostly steady on my feet, when I looked across the street and thought: hmm, is that a new pet store?"

Marisa was getting a bad feeling about this already.

"Anyway, it was their grand opening, and they were giving away free animals! All kinds of animals—puppies, kittens, some hamsters, a few ferrets—I think I saw a budgerigar in there. Isn't that a funny word, 'budgerigar'? What language is that even supposed to be? I guess maybe the parrot language . . ."

"Are you still drunk?" interrupted Marisa.

"A little, yes."

"You look like you've been crying."

"I haven't. Why would you—oh, right: the red eyes, the sniffles, the puffiness. Allow me to solve the mystery."

Gab went out of sight for a moment, into the hallway, and came back into the room carrying a dirty old cardboard box.

"Guess what's in here?"

Marisa looked at the box. The box meowed.

"Christ . . ."

"What? No, a kitty cat! And not just any cat, either—a Hemingway cat!"

Gab set the box down and opened the top flaps. A grey blur zipped low across the room, almost running headfirst into Marisa's feet and disappearing behind the torture rack in the gloom of Bovary's dungeon.

"She's going to love it here," Gab said. "It's a wonderfully enriched environment."

"A cat? You brought me a cat? I hate cats!"

"But it's a *polydactyl!* Six toes on each front paw. They're not like run-of-the-mill cats. They're more playful and codependent, kind of like dogs. Plus, it's already housebroken, so it poops in a box. I'd keep it myself, but I'm really allergic to cats."

"Take it back."

"I knew you would say that, with the baby coming and everything, but come on, cats don't *really* smother infants—"

"I'm not pregnant!" she blurted out.

Gab's jaw looked like it was about to hit his toes.

"It was a false alarm," she continued. "The home pregnancy test was wrong."

"Aren't they supposed to be 99% accurate?" asked Gab.

"And 1% inaccurate, evidently."

"Oh, right . . . Well! I guess we got lucky on that one. Huh. I'm not sure how to feel about this. I was looking forward to being a father."

"You're not ready to be a father. You're too impulsive, and you don't think even one step ahead."

"How so?"

A crash came from the dungeon, followed by a caterwaul.

"Oh," he said.

"Yeah, 'oh.' Gab, you know, with this whole pregnancy scare, I've been thinking . . . And I've decided that we can't see each other anymore."

"Fine. We'll start over again as friends."

"No. Not at all."

Gab stepped closer toward her. He could see that she was about to cry.

"But I love you," he said helplessly. "I thought we would be together. You know . . . for real. Not just as a fling. I thought you loved me, too. You said you did."

Marisa wanted to assure him, but found she could not.

"Gab, I have to end this."

"This? You mean us?"

"Yes. I can't do this anymore."

Gab forced himself not to pick up anything and hurl it across the room. It might scare her. He did not want that.

Suddenly, something rubbed against his leg. He looked down. The cat looked at him and immediately bit his ankle.

Maybe he was going to hurl something after all. He reached down to pick up the cat, but instead of throwing it pressed it to his chest.

"This is the right thing to do," said Marisa. "You deserve better. You deserve a nice, *single* girl who will love you and only you with all of her heart. You can be a real boyfriend—not just a fun distraction."

"A distraction?" Gab asked, petting the cat. The cat tilted back its head, purred, and bit his wrist.

"Gab, you know I can't give you what you deserve. I'm always looking over my shoulder. I'm always ashamed of myself when you leave."

"You're ashamed because you know you are depriving yourself of someone who would die for you," said Gab. "Marisa, please. Come with me. There doesn't have to be guilt or shame. You can choose love."

"I am. I married Phil because I loved him. I need to find that again. I think I owe that to him. I've been weak. I've taken the easy way out."

There was an uncomfortable pause.

"So I was just a distraction," Gab said eventually.

"I'm sorry." Marisa tucked her legs under herself on the couch and hugged a cushion to her chest, like Gab was doing with the cat.

Gab collected himself after a minute or so and chuckled—the kind of soft laugh reserved for defeat and, more than that, the acceptance of defeat.

It took him somewhat more time (and skin) to put the cat back into its box. Finally he shoved in the last of its wriggling appendages and closed the flaps. This small victory secured, he spoke up again.

"I guess this means I'll have to pack up Bovary's gear."

"Please do," Maria said. "I can make myself scarce for a couple of days."

"I love you, Marisa. That will be the last time I say it."

"Gab," she uttered as he picked up the box with the cat and walked out. She had no idea why she said anything at all. Maybe it was because she knew that once he left, Gab would be gone for good.

# Chapter 19

Pal's House — Deepwater, Texas

Pal entered his home to find Gab helping himself to a variety of foods in the kitchen. Judging by the jars and boxes open in front of him on the table, he was fixing one of his peanut butter and butter sandwiches, which always made Pal want to vomit just thinking about them.

"Where have you been?" Gab asked.

Pal flopped on the couch, put a pillow over his face and immediately pulled it away: the pillow smelled like feet. Probably Gab's feet, but Pal did not want to ask. It was definitely time to change the locks. He flung the pillow across the room.

"I've made a big mistake," he announced to everyone in the room, first and foremost himself.

"Hey, that's my line," laughed Gab. It was not Gab's usual laugh, which was an atrocious guffaw. This had nothing behind it.

"I guess I should be paying you royalties," said Pal.

"You know, I got a few calls on your phone this afternoon. Mistress Bovary says that you two need to talk about last night and this morning. I wrote her number down by the phone, in case you lost it. Wow, buddy, you move fast."

"I know," Pal groaned.

"And then, get this: your ex-fiancée called, too, and gave me—or you, rather—her new number. I wrote that one down right below Bovary's. She went on for a while about how she wants to talk, too, and that she didn't realize how passionate you were about her until you got into a fight over her at the coffee house. Which clears up the mystery of your face. What the hell happened there? But yeah, it sounds like she wants to jump you again. Hint: don't let her. Or maybe do let her. Maybe this time it'll work. But seriously, how about that? Everyone wants you. You're Mister Ladies' Man all of a sudden. Did you change your cologne or something?"

"Are you alright?" Pal asked, hearing new, harsh notes in Gab's voice.

"Yeah . . . yeah . . . I just need a nap. I've been up all night," Gab answered in an uncharacteristic mutter. "You're out of coffee, you know. I found a tin of green powder that calls itself tea on the top shelf, but I'm not loving it. It does not go well with my PB and B."

"Coffee is in the other cupboard." Pal said. "Behind the macaroni. Listen, be serious with me. Do you really think I should give her a second chance?"

"No."

"Then why did you tell me to let her jump me?"

"I said 'maybe let her.' Maybe is large; it contains multitudes. Do it. Don't do it. What does it matter, in the end? Anyway, she's evil. Don't do it. There. That's my final answer. Sorry. I'm just not thinking straight right now."

"So I shouldn't give her a second chance? But what if she's really changed? People change, Gab."

"Only in classical European literature of the second half of the 19th century and shitty romantic comedies. In real life, the people that change also change *back*."

"Then I guess they never really changed in the first place," Pal said, somewhat confused.

"I guess not," said Gab. "Fuck!" he roared suddenly and threw his cup in sink. The cup smashed. Two silent seconds later, Gab stormed out past him, muttering "g'night" under his breath.

For a while, Pal lay quietly, staring at the ceiling and not wondering about what just occurred or even acknowledging it. Then he picked up the note beside the phone and dialed one of the numbers, clearing his throat as he waited.

"Hey. It's Pal."

# Chapter 20

Marisa's Studio — The Heights, Houston, Texas

Dr. Sumner entered his wife's studio without knocking, walking in quietly through the door she left unlocked. Maybe he would startle her. That would teach her a lesson. She was always too trusting of people. What if one of the junkies he had seen across the street decided to pay her a visit? Him and all his buddies. If they beat her and raped her, would she learn how to lock her damn door then?

It was only the second time he had been inside the studio. He stared at the paintings leaned up against the wall and made a face. Same old waste of time and effort—though there were also a couple of weirder compositions he had not seen before, which he initially thought were the result of some sort of vandalism. Same awful furniture arranged without any thought to elegance: the chair, loveseat, and table Marisa had in her little apartment when she was still in school. She had refused to throw them out and let her husband of more than adequate means furnish the expensive studio with appropriately nice furniture. Sentimental nonsense.

There were some dividers bisecting the room. Phil walked around them and found himself looking at a darker space—this side of the studio had no windows—full of strange furniture and decorations hanging from the ceiling.

He stared, stupefied. Was he hallucinating? Were some kinds of parallel dimensions colliding and collapsing into one another? He took a few steps in and touched the torture rack. It was real. Was this whole fucking city into S&M?

"Phil? What are you doing here?"

He did not turn around.

"Well, well," he asked, feeling his neck tense up. "What have *you* been up to?"

"What are you doing back so soon?" his wife asked.

"I'll ask the questions!" he snapped. "What's with all the bondage shit? You turning the studio into a sex den?"

He turned to Marisa, who had her hands up defensively. What did she think he would do?

"I can explain. I thought you got in tomorrow."

"That is not an explanation," Phil said. "That is something a child would say."

Feeling very foolish and very old, the doctor picked up a studded paddle and hurled it against the wall, hoping to break it. It bounced off, almost hitting him in the face.

"I'm home early. Is that okay with you, Mrs. Sex Fiend? I understand, you didn't want me to surprise you while you were enjoying all this—" Phil picked up the cat-o'-nine that Gab had been so fond of. "What do you even call this?"

"I don't know. It's not mine."

"What the fuck is going on?"

"I'm helping a friend out with his business. Gab—you know Gab. He found this dominatrix named Mistress Bovary. We decided she could use some of my space, to cover a part of the—what's wrong?"

Phillip Barnes Sumner had walked slowly to the loveseat and sat down. He felt a swelling in his throat and a tightening in his stomach.

"I'm going home," he said after a long minute of silence, rising to his feet again.

# Chapter 21

Pal sat at the bar in the very café where he got pummeled by Buck Tadlock. The owner sat at the table adjacent, reading a *Houston Press*. Every minute or so he glanced at Pal. Pal tried not to make eye contact.

"Do I know you?" the owner finally asked.

"I don't think so," Pal said, still not looking at him.

"Oh, yes I do. You got into a fight here a few days ago. It had to be you. Look at your face."

Pal instinctively touched his bruised cheekbone, then realized what he was doing and quickly lowered his hand.

"I have a twin brother who comes here," he said.

"Oh, give me a break," said the owner before pointing at the door behind Pal. "And get out."

"Look, I'm scheduled to have heart surgery in a few days, and I'm just trying to save a relationship before I go in. She'll be here any minute. This is where we had our first date, sort of."

It was a long shot, but sometimes one had to gamble on the kindness of strangers.

"Is this where the strings come in?" asked the owner.

"It's a major procedure. They're going to kill off a part of my heart."

"Sounds routine to me. You know, they've really perfected these things in our day and age. My father had heart surgery three times."

"Really? How old is he?"

"Well, he's dead now. He died in a car accident coming home from the hospital."

"That doesn't make me feel better."

"I'm not trying to make you feel better. I'm asking you to get the fuck out. I make a living from this place. It can't acquire a reputation for fisticuffs. I cater to the art crowd, you know? Peaceful, civilized people. The boheme. Thin boys with no ass in scarves and glasses arguing over who is the more timeless: Modigliani or Picasso."

"Picasso," said Pal with confidence. He had no idea who Modigliani was.

"Right on. Although a year ago I would have argued Modigliani."

"*Three Musicians* is my favorite Picasso," Pal said, mentally thumbing through all the posters he had used in college to cover up cracks in his bedroom walls.

"I love that one, too. Those were the days, weren't they? You'll never have artists like him again—or Matisse, or Duchamp—even if you disagree with his methods. They have this big article here in the *Press* about pop art. I never got into that stuff. No soul. I guess anything with 'pop' in its title has no soul by definition, though."

"Pop bands can have soul. Not the manufactured boy bands, but some others."

"I did like the New Kids on the Block when I was in high school. Jordan and Jonathan Knight, be still my heart. Back to the issue at hand though—get out."

"Aw, come on," said Pal with a whine. "What about true love and overcoming all odds in the face of shit?"

The owner rolled his eyes.

"True love my big gay ass. All right, fine. Sit. Stay."

"Thanks," said Pal.

"Just so you know, if you would have said Modigliani, I would have called our mutual friend, that homophobic cop who dragged your cute ass out of here a few days ago, and told him you exposed yourself to my customers."

Pal looked around the uncharacteristically empty café. "What customers?"

"All right, me. You exposed yourself to me."

"Buy a boy a drink first," muttered Pal into his coffee.

Pal's ex walked in as the owner walked behind the counter.
She wasted little time.

"Hello, honey . . ."

"Hey, I didn't see you come in."

"Sorry I am late. I ran into you-know-who as I was leaving my place. He wanted the rest of his things and we—never mind. That's all in the past. Those were my green days."

"You mean salad days."

"What? Salad?"

"Yeah, like Cleopatra said of her days with Caesar."

"I don't know how the history books recorded it, Pally. And I don't care about some Egyptian bitch. I think you know what I meant. Anyway, let's not talk about my ex. Let's talk about us. You didn't happen to bring the ring by any chance?"

"The one you gave back to me? Why would I carry that thing around? I don't know why—"

"You said on the phone that we might be able to start over."

"Not from where we left off. I meant . . . maybe from the beginning."

"But I can still wear the ring, right? I remember it being . . . oh, how many carats?"

"A little less than one," Pal reminded her.

"Not bad," the owner of the café said as he eavesdropped like a pro from behind the counter.

"For now," the ex said, and she and the owner laughed a little too loudly for Pal's taste. It was a small thing, but it was enough. Pal decided to terminate both relationships. He would miss Café Comitatus.

"Excuse me," he said, rising from his chair.

"Where are you going?"

"I left something in the car."

"Okay. Hurry back. I'm starving," Pal's ex said as she perused the chalkboard menu.

# Chapter 22

"Bov! I need to talk to you!" shouted Pal in between gasps as he banged on Bovary's door. He had run up the stairs to reach her apartment because he could not wait for the elevator.

Mistress Bovary set down her bowl of salad and took a whip down from its nail on the wall. Someone was pounding like mad on the door and screaming indistinctly. She looked though the door peephole and saw Pal's sweat-beaded face.

"Palestrina!" she exclaimed, opening the door. "Damn it, you scared the hell out of me! Whatever happened to knocking gently? Where's the fire?"

"I need to come in," Pal said, wondering why she had answered the door with a riding whip in her hand.

"Come in, then. I'm making chicken and green salad for dinner. You like baked chicken?"

Bovary walked back into the kitchen and laid the whip on the counter. Pal closed the door and watched her for a moment.

"I'm sorry I said all those things. They were wrong."

"No, they weren't," she said, picking up the salad tongs again. "I mean, you could've handled it better, but I can't blame you. That's why I called you—to explain everything."

"You don't have to explain."

"Yes, I do. I don't want you to repress all this, dwell on it in silence for a few months, then suddenly bolt from here. I'd rather you knew exactly what happened."

"Uh huh." Pal wasn't really following her. He was distracted by the whip on the counter. It was giving him improper thoughts.

"A little tell-all, okay? Color yourself privileged. If you decide to leave after I tell you all about my past, please, don't come back any more. If you decide to stay, we'll have dinner, and then we can test-drive my new Egyptian cotton sheets. If you want to sleep over, there's a brand new toothbrush in my bathroom. I must warn you: if you decide to use it, we are in this for the long haul. Got it? Those are the rules. My rules. I am very ready for some normalcy in my life."

Pal smiled.

"No need for the story. Let's go confirm the thread count on those sheets." He leaned over the counter and took her by the hand, rubbing the inside of her palm with his thumb.

"It's actually only about three hundred," she mumbled. The touch was making her lightheaded. "But they're ELS: extra long staple . . ."

Pal leaned over a few more inches and kissed her.

Some time later, on the cusp of what promised to be a magnificent night of passion, they were interrupted by the smell of burning chicken.

It took them an hour to rid the apartment of lingering smoke. After disaster was avoided, they crawled back into bed.

"Well, that was romantic," Bovary said. "Although you did look really cute running around half-naked and fanning the smoke detectors."

"Any more surprises?"

"Other than the gimp in my closet? Nah."

"Good. I've felt my heart come out of my chest enough these past few days."

The bedroom fell silent.

"When are you going to the hospital?"

"In two days—the day after Halloween. Why?"

"I want to come. I want to be by your side."

"I'd rather you didn't. If people are around, I'll just get more nervous. Besides, the doctor says there is nothing to worry about. It's a routine procedure. They've perfected it. I'll tell you what: give me this one, and the next time I have to go to the hospital, you can come. And you can even bring our kids and grandkids."

The two fell asleep without ever having sex. Before she dozed off, Bovary placed her ear to Pal's chest and counted his heartbeats.

# Chapter 23

Lutheran Hospital — Medical Center, Houston, Texas

Gab entered the hospital holding a six-pack of St. Arnold's. He made no effort to hide the contraband as he strolled down the hallway looking for his best friend's room. No one working at the hospital seemed to notice anyway. This left Gab somewhat disappointed.

"Did someone order a party?!" he sang out as he walked into the private room, waking up Pal, who had been enjoying a linear dream where he and Bovary married, had children, and were still having amazing sex in their old age.

"Is that beer? You can't bring beer in here," Pal said, stretching under the thin hospital blanket.

"Says who? I didn't see any sign. Besides, they've got loads of shit in this place that will get you way more fucked up than beer. Think of this as pre-gaming."

"You're three sheets to the wind."

"I'm worried sick! Come on, have one beer with me. Or else I'll be four sheets to the wind. Or five. I'm going to run out of sheets, Pal. I can't be out of sheets—I'm driving!"

"You're not driving. Please tell me you're not. I don't need to be worrying about you on top of everything else. I'm a nervous wreck as it is."

As Pal heard these words come out of his mouth, he realized he wasn't actually that nervous. Bovary had just called, trying once again to convince him to let her come to the hospital. He ordered her to stay away, not wanting her to hover and worry as he went into the operating room.

Pal clinked beer bottles with his friend.

"Here's to a shot at Purgatory," Gab said before guzzling half the beer at once.

"I'm an atheist," said Pal sourly.

"How many times do we have to go over this? You're not an atheist: you're an agnostic. Atheists actively disbelieve in everything. You must believe in something out there after . . . you know . . . after all this."

"I don't think I ever have," Pal said. He had never concerned himself with the afterlife. He was always too busy living—or rather, existing—to prepare himself for the eternal sleep and what dreams may come in it.

"Come on."

"Actually, now that I really think about it, I know I never have. I was just never into religion as a concept. Seemed like if you committed to putting your faith in God, you might get some comfort out of it, but the trade-off was that God could do whatever He pleased to you, like take away someone you love. Maybe it was the wrong choice, I don't know. Look at where playing it safe has got me. What if I never come out of this?"

"For fuck's sake, Pal. Don't talk like that."

"You know, Gab, you're just like me."

"No way. I'm the impulsive one, you're the practical one. That's how it's always been."

"Okay, I'll give you that, but deep inside—don't give me that look—deep inside, we're the same. You fancy yourself a gambler, but you only go for the sure thing, which is whatever suits your needs at any given time."

Gab managed to spit his beer back into the bottle. It wasn't the right time or place for a spit-take.

"What the hell are you talking about? Have they started pumping drugs into you already?"

"Let me ask you this: why do you pursue a married woman?"

This was a strange new Palestrina. The old one usually kept his nose out of other people's personal lives. What went on between Gab and Marisa had nothing to do with him. Besides, who was he to play holier-than-thou? His new crush was a dominatrix.

"You've seen Marisa. She's gorgeous," said Gab nervously, eager to change the subject. But Pal was too focused.

"Come on, Gab. There are thousands of gorgeous girls out there. And many of them are even willing to date you, God only knows why. Why are you so set on her?"

"I don't know," mumbled Gab. Pal was, to say the very least, freaking him out. Also, the buzz from the three beers he had consumed in as many minutes was making it hard to focus.

"Answer me. Why her?"

"Come on, man. Enough with the Spanish Inquisition, okay?"

Pal waited for a few long seconds, then said mercilessly:

"It's because you know she will never leave her husband. You two are never going to be in a serious relationship. Somehow that comforts you, never really having her. It's your way of never losing anyone close to you—again."

"That's a hell of a thing to say to me, and here of all places. You think I wanted to come here?"

"I understand, but listen to me, damn it. For once, listen to me. You have to go for something real. You can't keep avoiding life. I know how it is. I didn't date for ages after getting my engagement ring thrown back in my face. But you can't stay out on the sidelines for the rest of your life because you are afraid of losing someone again. You deserve good things, man. A real career instead of all this get-rich-quick nonsense. A happy marriage instead of being a married woman's boy toy."

"Hey, Pal, I know exactly what I want and what I deserve. And guess what? It doesn't involve working fifty-hour weeks at a desk in front of a computer, killing my eyes and my back and my will to live, being forced to put in free overtime so that some CEO upstairs can buy another boat, another car, another house, another girlfriend, or a fucking show dog. You know damn well that isn't me. I want something else. I just don't know what it is yet. It hasn't come to me yet. But I'm going to keep trying, keep looking until I find it. That's not playing it safe, not the way I see it."

Gab finished his fourth beer, backwash and all. The nice buzz he had built up was gone.

There was an awkward silence in the room, something very rare when the two friends were together. Pal waited a bit, then spoke again.

"Okay, but what about your personal problems?"

"The ones that are none of your business?"

"The ones you keep making my business. I don't mind. I really don't. But maybe I should have guided you, given you more advice."

Gab opened the fifth and last beer.

"Well, okay," he said. "I confide in you. So what? I don't expect anything. I don't need advice. I just need to vent."

"So everything is supposed to be one way? You can emote at me for years, but you don't want to hear my analysis?"

"Analysis? Oh, brother," Gab said.

"Maybe you're right. Maybe this is none of my business. But when you finally get it together and get married, you know your wife will expect you to listen to her. You might as well start getting used to it now."

"I'm never getting married," Gab said matter-of-factly, dropping on the chair next to the bed and groaning. "Watching that psycho bitch crush your heart cured me of any desire to marry. And you actually wanted to settle down."

"Never?" Pal asked.

"Look at married people. Are they happy? They say they are, but look at them when they say it. Their mouth says 'It's been a magical ride,' but their eyes say 'For the love of God, someone stop this thing, I want to get off!' People who tell me they hate their jobs say it with much more enthusiasm than people who tell me they are happy in their marriage."

Gab reclined in the chair, satisfied.

"What is your favorite movie?" Pal asked after Gab got comfortable.

"*Roadhouse*. You know that."

"I'm not convinced. You didn't say that with much enthusiasm. Do you really think it's your favorite? Maybe you hate movies altogether."

Gab laughed.

"Touché."

When the nurse came in to check up on Pal, she found Pal in good spirits and Gab asleep in the chair with empty beer bottles scattered around him.

"You there! Are you crazy, boy? You can't be bringing no beer in here!" she said.

"Huh? Wha—? Right, no beer. Right on, m'am. No beer here. They're all empty, see?"

Gab turned one of the bottles upside down and immediately soaked his pants.

"Give me that!" the nurse said. She took the bottles, threw them into the small wastebasket, and took the wastebasket out of the room.

Pal smiled as Gab tried to dab the beer from his crotch with the bottom of his T-shirt.

"Think about what I said," Pal said.

"Yeah, sure. Are you going to finish your beer?"

Pal looked down and noticed he still had a half-full bottle tucked between his elbow and ribs.

"Be my guest," he said, handing the bottle to Gab. "You already wet yourself—why bother holding back now?"

# Chapter 24

Lutheran Hospital — Medical Center, Houston, Texas

Marisa entered a surgical prep room. She hadn't wanted to meet her husband in a hospital of all places, but he had insisted. It had been a strange phone call, and Marisa was apprehensive about his sudden desire to have a potentially messy tête-à-tête at his sterile workplace, but in light of recent events, nothing surprised her.

"Marisa, I'd like to say a few things," Phil said right away as she walked in. He sounded like an attorney beginning a cross-examination. She could tell he had been waiting impatiently for her to arrive. She prepared herself for the crescendo of his voice.

"I have some things to say, too," she replied.

She looked into his eyes. It looked like he had been crying. Of course, she couldn't be sure: she had seen his eyes red when he couldn't sleep, and when he broke his nose in a charity basketball game. But this red seemed different somehow.

"Please, hear me out first." He shifted to a gentle, cautious tone that she was not used to.

"I always have," she said.

"Yes, I know. And I know this isn't the best place to discuss these things, but I had to see you as soon as possible."

"Do you want a divorce? Is that what this is about? You can ask me. I won't make a scene," Marisa said.

"I thought you were going to hear me out."

"I'm tired of doing what you want all the time. You think it's easy being a trophy wife? As long as I look good, stay out of your way, and act devoted and happy at your social functions, you don't even care what happens to me. We don't do anything romantic. We hardly even have sex anymore, Phil."

"There's a reason for that."

"I know I didn't turn out to be what you wanted," she said. Now that she had started talking, it was hard to stop until she had gotten everything off her chest. "I can't change who I am, and you must have known that. Why did you even marry me? Why put me through these years of hell?"

"I didn't know at the time. I thought if I gave you an alternative to being a starving art student—if I gave you everything you could want, I would make you happy. But you just threw all my efforts back in my face. I became—"

Phil searched for the right word. This was more than he had said to her in months, and realizing that had suddenly made him incredibly sad.

"I became bitter," he said finally. "I mean, can you really . . ."

"I've been seeing someone else, Phil. For about a year now. And I'm pregnant. The baby could be his, or it could be yours. I don't know," she blurted out all at once. It came out all a-jumble. Then again, there was no proper way to admit such things.

Seconds ticked by in silence. Phil closed his eyes, anticipating a dull pain to invade his heart and linger within him forever after. He knew already that years from now there would still be nights when he would lie sleepless, thinking of this moment.

"Why would you tell me this?" he whispered.

"I know, it's horrible, but it's the truth."

"Marisa, my God. Don't tell me this."

"I'm not leaving you for him. But I am leaving you. I need to live my own life."

"Why? Why . . . did you . . ." The words dripped off of his tongue only slightly faster than melting glass.

"I wanted—"

Dr. Sumner struck his wife's face hard with the palm of his hand, like he had often seen his father do to his mother. He was surprised how easily it came to him.

Marisa fell to the floor.

"Phil . . . don't," she pleaded softly, shielding her face with her hands.

It was the softness of her voice that made him realize what he had done.

"Get out . . . please . . . get out," he said.

Marisa lowered her hands and saw her husband on his knees staring at the floor. She lifted herself up, backed out of the room, and left in a hurry.

"Doctor?"

A resident was speaking to him softly. Marisa was long gone. Dr. Sumner sat cross-legged on the floor, looking like he was meditating.

"I'm coming," he said.

Dr. Sumner finished prepping and walked into the operating room. He was met with stares, most of which were immediately diverted.

"Are you okay?" said one young female assistant with audible compassion as she handed him the angiogram and echocardiogram.

"Get out of my operating room," he said calmly.

The assistant left.

Dr. Sumner looked around at each of his staff to see if they got his point. No one spoke up.

He looked over the angiogram and echocardiogram mechanically.

"Looks like we're good to go. Patient ready?"

Dr. Sumner proceeded with the ablation procedure, using a magnetic guidance system to thread the catheter up through the groin to the heart. He had done this so many times before, it was almost reflex. All that was left was to identify the proper artery and inject the alcohol into the obstructive tissue to induce a controlled heart attack.

He tried to maintain focus through the haze of his emotions. "Rational thought always follows emotional reactions," he mumbled beneath his mask. Already he could feel his catecholamine levels drop; his adrenaline rush was subsiding. Of course, it would take him a certain amount of time to metabolize all the chemicals released when his wife told him the news, but the peak was cleared. He was returning to his familiar world of reason.

"Dr. Sumner," he thought he heard someone say.

Certainly, he handled the situation with Marisa well. He didn't even slap her that hard, though perhaps he should have. What would another man have done if he heard his wife admit she might be pregnant with someone else's child? The situation was incomprehensible. He might not have been the ideal husband, but he didn't deserve this.

"Dr. Sumner," he heard a voice again, more urgent this time.

No, he had to be honest with himself. He had been far less than an ideal husband. He deceived his wife first: he had a mistress. He supported a mistress and her decadent occupation to satisfy his own carnal desires. He had let himself be taken by bestial ecstasy and mistook it for love. How wrong he had been! But now it was too late. Marisa probably sensed it, and that's why she found someone else as well. He had made his bed.

"Doctor!"

Someone pushed Dr. Sumner out of the way. He leaned against the wall, propping himself up with his forearm. As soon as he felt able, he walked out of the operating room. Other people rushed past him—into the room, not out.

Phil wandered the hallways until a nurse caught up with him and escorted him to an empty room.

"Doctor, please, lie down," the nurse said.

"I made the bed," he said to the nurse.

"Yes, doctor, of course you did. You made the bed. Now please, lie down."

"Yes," said Phil. "I have to lie in my bed."

He knew what had to be done. Minutes later, he fell into a deep sleep.

# Chapter 25

Marisa's Studio – The Heights, Houston, Texas

Gab and Bovary cleaned out the dungeon in silence, picking up the S&M gear and placing it neatly into boxes. Both wanted to be somewhere else, which happened to be the same place: next to Pal as he recovered.

"Bov, I'm sorry about all of this. I honestly thought it was a great idea. I guess it was doomed from the start. I shouldn't have mixed business with my personal affairs."

"I know you meant well."

"Yeah," Gab said solemnly. He only wished Pal had not been involved. He had let him down so many times already.

"It's all a big mess, isn't it? What are we going to do now? Bring all this stuff back to your apartment?"

"I have to vacate that place, too. The guy I used to be with that was helping me out with the rent busted me with Pal and wasn't too keen on the idea of another man on his turf. I can't afford the place on my own."

"Well, we have to do something about that. Maybe we can room together—if you and Pal don't elope or something."

"You'd have to use these to get me to the altar," Bovary said, holding up a pair of handcuffs. "But you might be a good roomie. Pal says you're never at your loft."

"He's right. I think he's getting sick of me crashing on his sofa all the time. But I can't really sleep at my place. The jukebox in the bar below plays Clarence Carter's 'Strokin'' all night long. Apparently, that guy strokes it to the East *and* to the West."

"Actually, I already have a place in mind. No loud honky tonk downstairs, even," she said. "Let's take a break."

Gab sat down on the floor. Bovary sat down beside him.

"I noticed you didn't say your ex's name. You're like Pal in that way."

"Yeah, my ex is not a nice guy. I thought he was, once upon a time. To me, at least. You know how people are when they're in a new relationship: everyone's on their best behavior. It doesn't last."

"No, it doesn't," agreed Gab.

"So, you and Marisa . . . ?"

"She's the one who ended it, and she's right. It's better for both of us. I'm just worried that her husband is never going to change. I don't want that for her."

Gab pressed his index finger and thumb to his eyelids.

Bovary said nothing as she wrapped one arm around him tightly, as if holding him against a coming wind gust.

"I'm okay," he said. "Let's think happy thoughts, listen to happy music . . ."

Gab walked over to Bovary's old portable stereo and looked at the CD cases around it. There was nothing but classical, which he thought was a bit odd for dungeon music. He picked a CD up at random and put it in the player. When the first notes sounded, Gab perked up and turned up the volume.

"I love this one! Always cheers me up. What's it called?" he asked, raising his voice over the music.

"Hell if I know," Bovary yelled back, standing up to finish packing. "I just got it for the ambience."

Gab pulled out his phone and began to mock-conduct the invisible orchestra with it. A minute or so later, it dawned on him that his "baton" was vibrating. He flipped the phone open and put it to his ear.

Bovary, whose back had been turned to Gab, heard nothing over the blaring music and did not realize he was on the phone at all until he hurled it at the wall, smashing it to pieces.

|PART THREE| November 2002

# Chapter 26

On her way to the house she shared with Dr. Sumner, Marisa drove past River Oaks, down Kirby, and through Rice Village. At the stop signs she stared at the people walking from shop to shop, buying shoes, sweaters, and expensive nonfat cappuccinos. Once upon a time she had looked at these people with amazement, singling out the obviously rich, wondering what it would be like to have a life that included spa days. Now she longed for the days when she was envious of the wealthy. Knowing there was a bunch of neglected women and betrayed men in this city made reflecting on her own life that much harder.

She pulled into the driveway and walked though the side door that led into the kitchen. Phil was waiting for her, sitting at the breakfast table with a dozen yellow roses in front of him. He got up and walked toward her.

"These are for you," he said.

"I don't understand," said Marisa.

"I don't want a divorce."

Marisa took the roses and walked over to the cabinet to find a vase. Phil waited for her to say something. After a few distracted glances over the shelves, she gave up her search and laid the roses on the counter. Phil resumed talking.

"I wanted to tell you something in the hospital, but . . . things happened. What I wanted to say was . . . well . . . I haven't been faithful to you, either."

"I assumed that much," she said, although she had not. She had been too wrapped-up in her own infidelity to even consider that her husband could be doing the same thing on his end.

"I want us to start over. I had wanted to tell you all of this before, but you . . . beat me to the punch, so to speak."

"I know I probably should have told you at some other time and place, but you really didn't give me much of a choice. You forbade me to sleep at my own house, for Christ's sake."

"I know," he said. "I know I brought much of this on myself. Now I'm in danger of losing you. I know this isn't what you want to hear, but now that I feel like it's all over, I want you that much more. I'm trying to be honest here."

"What about the child? Doesn't that change things for you? I think you're still in a state of shock. You're not thinking clearly."

"We'll raise it together whether it's mine or not. This way, we can make up for the sins we've committed. In a strange way, wouldn't it be good for us?"

She had not seen him make this kind of effort in years, not since their courtship. However, the wounds ran too deep this time around.

"So you're saying you'd gladly be a father to this child, even if it's not yours?"

"I believe there are bigger things at play here. I'm not saying it will be easy."

Marisa didn't want to believe they were marionettes in a lustful performance controlled by God. God wouldn't ruin lives to get a point across.

"I can't be a good wife to you. I cheated on you, and you've just admitted you cheated on me," she said. "We make for a pretty pathetic couple."

Phil paced around the kitchen, crossing into the den and stopping short of the paint stain on the rug. He thought back to when he first caught glimpse of it.

"I'm leaving town for awhile," he said. "Maybe a couple of weeks, maybe a month."

"Leaving town?"

"Nothing to do with us. Something happened at the hospital."

"What happened?"

"I'll tell you later. But the ranch sounds really good right now. I'm going there to sort things out, clear my head. I don't expect you to come with me."

So this is how he is going to deal, Marisa thought. By running away from everything to his ranch. She couldn't blame him. She thought about skipping town, too.

"I mean, I'd like for you to come with me," he continued. "I don't know if it's the right thing for us to do, going away together, but it feels right. This can be our new beginning. If we atone for our mistakes . . . that's all that matters, right?"

Marisa stared at him, speechless. He could see a small bruise near her eye.

"Of course . . . well . . ." Phil sounded tremendously uncomfortable. "If we do call it quits, I will take care of you. I won't leave you out in the street."

"I don't want anything from you," Marisa said, then corrected herself. "I don't deserve anything from you. I abandoned you. It's only fair for you to abandon me as well."

Phil had never known a woman to hold herself this accountable for the end of a relationship. He had pushed her away, ignored her, and neglected her, and yet she still accepted most or all of the blame.

"Do you still love me?" he asked her.

"I don't know, Phil. I need time. Things are extremely complicated now. I think you can't or don't want to admit to yourself how serious all this is."

Phil thought of Jessica and how he flew back from Prague and rushed straight away to see her. He thought of her face, and how her eyes had been so different than he remembered when she opened the door to see him. So full of life.

He thought of the patient on the operating table and remembered the panic in the room. He remembered walking out after the confusion, hearing people shout after him, the nurse finally grabbing him in the hall as the returning assistant and the chief of medicine ran past him into the operating room to address the code blue.

Phil looked at the paint stain on the rug again. It was much, much smaller than he remembered.

"I forgive you, Phil," said Marisa. "I do. But it may be too late for us."

"I understand," he said.

"I'll come back tomorrow morning, okay? We can talk then."

"Okay."

Marisa left the house without saying another word.

# Chapter 27

Pal's House — Deepwater, Texas

Pal's father sat motionless in a chair next to his wife, who was scowling at Gab. She was not one to hide her feelings. If Gab remembered correctly, she was not one to defend her actions, either.

Pal's mother came back for the second time just as Pal was starting high school. She arrived one morning at the home she had purchased with his father over a decade earlier and began cooking breakfast as though nothing had happened.

As Pal and his father ate the rubbery eggs and the burnt pancakes, they listened to Mrs. Thomas's big plans for the family. She wanted them to move out of Deepwater. The town was haunted, she said. She handed Pal and his father several flyers advertising town homes near Memorial Park. Pal gave their floor plans a cursory glance; his father studied them more thoroughly.

"I always thought it would be nice to live inside the loop," his father said. "We would be closer to the university. I wouldn't have to drive that far to the campus."

In the years following his wife's departure, the only thing that got him up in the morning was knowing he might turn another apathetic college kid into a classical music fan with his lectures on Rachmaninoff and Liszt and all the greats. The only thing that got him to sleep at night was a liberal dose of Scotch.

Now his wife was back after years of separation from her family, sitting across from the two Thomas men and acting as though she never left.

Pal decided then and there that he had no more use for the odd couple and began planning his escape, which mostly boiled down to attending a college in Austin, or altogether out of state.

Gab had only met Pal's mother a few times, yet even that handful of encounters made obvious her animosity towards him. This confused him. Gab rubbed countless people the wrong way, but he was usually a big hit with parental units.

Pal's mother had always wondered why her son, who seemed to have all of his faculties about him, chose Gab as a confidant. She was asking herself this question again today, having learned that this flibbertigibbet was the named executor of her son's last will and testament.

Gab wondered things, too—for instance, why a woman with such a long list of shortcomings was not more accepting of other people's faults. In fact, that was just what he told her as she lobbied aggressively for a lavish funeral, against her dead son's own wishes.

Pal's mother calmly asked him what that statement was supposed to mean. Gab calmly told her it meant that her son was a far better person than she could either hope to be or even understand.

"Pal wanted a small service and a cremation."

"He'll be buried next to his grandmother and grandfather," Pal's mother insisted. Pal's father remained silent.

"Look, I agreed to have the service at the funeral home you picked out, but he wanted to be cremated, Mrs. Thomas. I want to honor that."

"He will not be burned like garbage. He is my son, and I will not have anyone tell me what he wanted. How would you know what he wanted? You just used him!"

Gab looked at Pal's father. Mr. Thomas sat very still in his chair, and there was no color in his face. Gab wondered if there would be two funerals tomorrow.

"Mr. Thomas?" he called out hesitantly.

The old man did not stir. He kept looking down while the matriarch of the Thomas family continued to speak.

"He agrees with me! My son will be buried in the family plot. I don't care what it says in those papers in your hand. You will do what's right. It's the least you can do for ruining his life all of these years. My son was a beautiful boy, but he was a terrible judge of character."

"Must run in the family," muttered Gab, still looking at the paterfamilias playing dead in the leather chair. "Fuck it. Fine. Bury him. Buy a fancy coffin covered with flowers and make the house of death so fucking phenomenally pretty that all those neighbors you want to impress will shit themselves. Whatever takes your mind off the inconvenient truth that my best friend—the one you abandoned when he was a baby, in case you've forgotten—is fucking dead. Satisfied?"

Pal's mother smirked and tapped Mr. Thomas on the shoulder—a signal for him to get up and leave with her.

"*Quite* satisfied," she said as she and her husband departed.

When he heard the front door close, Gab flung the will across the room and leaned back in his chair.

"I'm sorry, Pal," he said. "I tried."

# Chapter 28

Forest Lawn Memorial Funeral Home – Deepwater, Texas

Gab arrived at the funeral home early and asked to be led into the room where Pal lay. He held his breath as the director opened the double doors leading into the spacious room. Out of the double-hung windows, Gab could see the oak trees lining the cemetery. He could also see the headstones.

"Um, could we close the curtains?" Gab said, pointing to the windows. "I kind of want to forget where I am right now."

"Of course. Here, allow me," said the funeral director.

"Can I have a moment alone after you do that?"

With the curtains closed, the atmosphere in the room turned gloomy and ominous. Two lamps on end tables provided a little yellow light. The director walked toward the light switch to turn on the overhead fluorescents.

"No, it's fine like this," Gab said.

"Of course. Is everything else to your liking?"

Gab had not even looked at the casket and floral arrangements when he walked in. He looked at Pal lying in the coffin and quickly turned back toward the director.

"I'm sure everything is fine," Gab said.

"Excellent. I think it looks wonderful."

An odd choice of adjective, Gab thought. Nothing looks wonderful in this place.

"A moment, please?" reminded Gab.

The director closed the doors as he left. Gab inched closer to his friend, reluctant to stand beside the coffin. When he did, he noticed they had put Pal in a bright red tie, which he would have hated. Pal never wore ties, even to important functions. It was one of his little rebellions against society, Gab speculated.

"Hey," he began after staring at Pal for a while. "I feel stupid standing here talking to you. I don't know what to say, really. I don't even know if you can hear me. You're probably loving that."

He drew a deep breath.

"They put a tie on you. It doesn't look that bad. I guess you should be presentable at your own funeral. It's the least you could do."

Gab reached and touched Pal's hand. The shock of its coldness made him jump a bit. He didn't know why—death's peculiarities were not exactly foreign to him.

"Sorry, brother. Got a little freaked out." Gab placed his hand back on Pal's. "Your mom, she's a piece of work. She railroaded me into burying you. In the end, I figured, what the hell, right? What do you care now? Maybe I should've fought her harder. I hope that doesn't make me a bad executor. I was just so . . . tired."

Gab was interrupted by a thumping noise. It sounded like there was a washing machine with an unbalanced load somewhere in another room in the building.

"I wish I could ask you one more question," he continued. "I wish a lot of things. I wish I had taken you more seriously at the hospital, that I had listened to you more often. I wish I were a better person. I'm a fuck-up. I leave a trail of hurt wherever I go. You never hurt anyone."

Gab heard the thumping again but tried to ignore it as he spoke.

"You were a good person surrounded by bad people. Maybe your mom was right. Maybe I did ruin your life. Sometimes I wonder myself."

The thumping came again, stronger this time. He could now tell it was coming from just outside the window, the noise muffled by the thick curtains. Letting go of his friend's hand, Gab walked toward the noise, which was now relentless.

Sunlight flooded the room as he opened the curtains. It took a moment for his eyes to adjust, and then he saw a cardinal flying into the window and violently bumping against the glass.

Gab cracked open the window to shoo the suicidal son of a bitch away, or better yet, smack him. But once the window was open just wide enough for Gab to push his arm through, the bird flew inside, across the room, and landed on Pal.

"Holy shit!" Gab said. "Get! Scat!"

He tried not to shout as he flailed his arms and walked toward the casket. The bird paid him no mind. It started to peck and pull at Pal's chest.

"Hey! Quit it!" shouted Gab.

He took off his blazer and held it like a matador wielding a cape in front of the bull about to charge. The cardinal kept at its business—pecking at Pal's chest. Had he not been so upset, Gab would have found it hilarious.

"Get off him!"

When Gab was almost within jacket-throwing range, the cardinal flapped its wings and flew in a tight circle above the casket. Gab threw his coat up in the air. The blazer missed the bird; however, it did not miss the floral arrangement on top of the coffin.

"Great. Can this get any worse?" Gab said.

As if to answer him, the cardinal shat directly on the casket and flew back out the open window.

For a moment, Gab stood in silence and tried to absorb what had just happened. Then he walked over to the casket and examined the huge glob of white bird shit. He didn't think such a little creature could shit so much. It really was a lot of shit.

He looked at Pal. The bird had practically pulled Pal's tie out from underneath his suit. Gab started to push it back beneath the buttoned jacket and smooth it out. The bird's beak had left noticeable indentions in the fabric.

"Damn, Pal. That bird really did a number on you . . ."

Gab stopped, snorted, and tried to untie the tie. The tie came off in his hand.

"A clip on? Cheap bastards."

"Is everything okay in here?" asked the funeral director, appearing quietly and unobtrusively at the door, as if summoned by Gab's half-mumbled complaint.

Gab held the bright red tie in his hand.

"A few changes. One—no tie. By the way, seriously, a clip on?"

The funeral director almost shrugged, Gab was sure.

"And two—we're going with cremation after the service tomorrow."

"Of course," the funeral director said, staring at the floral arrangement lying upended on the ground and the smear of what appeared to be thick white paint on the casket. "I trust you are aware that the casket is nonrefundable?"

# Chapter 29

Forest Lawn Memorial Funeral Home — Deepwater, Texas

It was a nice service. Pal's father gave an unexpectedly moving eulogy, talking with feeling about all the years he and his son looked out for one another after his mother left. Pal's mother sat with her mouth hanging open, but Pal's father kept on going without missing a beat.

Gab rose from his seat and hugged Pal's father as he stepped down from the podium. Pal's mother watched the embrace with distain.

"Thank you for understanding about the cremation," he whispered in the man's ear. "It's what he wanted."

"I envy you," Pal's father whispered back. He tilted his head back and looked at Gab. His blank expression gave away nothing. He patted Gab on the shoulder and sat down next to his wife, who leaned over and started to complain about the eulogy.

"If I were you, I wouldn't," Pal's father said without looking at her. After a few seconds she crossed her arms and stared ahead in silence.

After the service, the music of Giovanni Palestrina played through the chapel speakers: *Missa Papai Marcelli* on repeat. The selection was the parents' choice. Apparently, Pal's father used to play the Mass for his young son on Sundays before the boy grew old enough to request something from the new wave of British bands—records his father did not own. Gab knew he himself would have probably chosen something inappropriately brash and loud, so he did not begrudge Pal's parents their music selection.

Everyone had left except Gab and Bovary. She stood in the back of the chapel; Gab sat in the front row near Pal with his head bowed.

Bovary had not wanted to be that close to the casket, but she walked up and sat next to Gab.

"He wanted to be cremated," said Gab. "His parents wanted him buried."

"What did you want?" she asked.

"What did I want? I didn't want to let him down. I didn't want to cause a conflict, either. I guess I can't have everything. Anyway, I'm going through with his wishes. I told his parents. His dad is cool with it. I don't give a shit what his mother thinks."

"Sounds like you, wanting *almost* everyone to be happy," Bovary said. "I'm sure he can see all of this, and I bet he doesn't mind. It's probably all silly to him at this point."

"Strange that I had to decide all this. I didn't think he'd name me as the executor of his will. I didn't even realize he had a will! How fucked up is that? Not even thirty and he had a will."

"It's not that weird. He was prepared, that's all."

"I guess he knew death could happen at any time. You know, he really helped me out when my parents passed away."

"Well, he loved you. He wanted to take care of you. And he knew you'd take care of him now."

It seemed odd to Bovary that she was so calm. Perhaps the reality had not set in yet. She could have loved this man who was now dead. How long had it been? Was it really only a few days? She had no idea how to feel, how to behave. She felt guilty being there among the people who had known Pal for years, but she also felt it was her place to help out the people who knew him and loved him most. They were, after all, an extension of Pal.

And she was also grateful, thankful that love was out there. For that, she felt no guilt.

"Well, I wish I would've known he was going to leave me all his stuff," Gab said. "I might've treated him better when he was alive. I mean, Jesus! His car is paid off, and it only has twelve thousand miles on it. Not a bad score."

Gab laughed suddenly. It resounded from the high chapel ceiling. Gab wondered if anyone had laughed that loudly in there before.

"You okay?" asked Bovary.

Gab nodded.

"Gallows humor. It's all I ever had. All I will ever have, I guess."

"I beg to differ. You also have a friend who's a dominatrix. Not every boy can boast that. I'll hire you on as an assistant. You can take my devil suit to the dry cleaners. Disinfect the restraints."

Gab laughed again. It was comforting to laugh at someone else's jokes for a change. Bovary draped her arm around him and kissed his forehead.

There were footsteps on the tile floor behind them. Bovary turned around.

"She's here, Gab," she said, turning back around. "I should leave you two alone. I'll be outside."

Gab turned and saw Marisa. She was beautiful in black. She was beautiful in anything.

"Thanks, Bov," he said, putting his head down again. "I don't think this will take long."

In the end, Bovary did not look at Pal. She did not want to remember him that way. On her way out, she embraced Marisa. They said nothing to one another.

Marisa approached Gab cautiously and placed a gentle hand on his tense shoulder.

"How are you holding up?" she asked.

"Okay," he said. "Ish."

Marisa sat down next to him.

"You're not okay."

Gab took her hand, removed it from his shoulder and placed it gently on her lap, holding it a while.

"No, I'm not. I'm devastated," he said, letting it go.

Marisa placed her hand back on Gab's shoulder, then around his arm, more tightly than Bovary had done.

"I'm here for you," she said. "Whatever you need."

Gab did not look up. He was afraid to.

"Leave your husband and be with me," he said simply.

Marisa removed her hand on her own this time.

"I'm not going to leave him."

She was starting to explain, but Gab interrupted her. He didn't need to hear anything else.

"Go," he said.

"What?"

"Please, go."

"Gab, stop. Listen to me."

"I don't need you here. I don't want to be reminded that I've lost two people that I loved one after the another," Gab said. "Again."

"I don't know what to say."

Gab had to look at her once more.

"Don't say anything, Marisa. Just do me one favor, just promise me one thing."

"Anything," she said.

"Find that girl I met that night in the pub. Do you remember her at all? I've never forgotten her. She was so passionate about art, philosophy, life. She didn't care about what other people thought. She had these big dreams, and she was going to do it all on her own. Promise me that you'll find her again. Promise me that."

Gab rose and went over to the casket, bowing over it for a minute or two. Then he walked out of the chapel without looking back.

For a while after Gab left, Marisa sat alone in the pew. Then she collected herself and also walked up to Pal's casket.

"Who's going to watch over him now?" she said, halfway expecting an answer.

# Chapter 30

After settling the bill with Forest Lawn—though it still puzzled him why they couldn't buy back the casket, even at a fraction of its price—Gab went to the Pot Callin' Kettle. It was his first time at the diner without Pal. He stood by the booth that he had always insisted they sit in, then slid into the vinyl seat, thinking of earlier days.

"Move over, Pal. Hur hur. Get it? Seriously though, move your ass over."

"Sit across from me," Pal said.

"There's a wad of gum stuck to the seat."

Pal threw his hands up.

"Then let's get another booth. You're not sitting next to me," he said as he tried to get up. Gab pushed his shoulder back down and forced his way into the booth.

"Just scoot over already. Don't be a baby."

Pal groaned his long, guttural growl.

"People are going to think we're a couple," he said.

"So what?" said Gab, looking around for a waitress.

"This is Deepwater, Gab," Pal whispered with a grumble that would have made Tom Waits proud. "This is the Pot Callin' Kettle, not the Pie Hole on Kirby. You are *not* sitting next to me on one side of a booth."

Gab forced his way even farther in, pushing Pal against the wall.

"Hey, stop it! People are already looking at us. Come on! What is so special about this booth?"

Gab made a counter-clockwise circle with his extended arms, hands open and palms down.

"The chi of this place flows mostly through this booth right here. It's special."

"You know what I am going to do? I'm going to throw out all those Zen Buddhism books of yours. Replace them with some real books, the kind that can really turn a life around."

"You mean your self-help books? What's the one you're reading now? *How to Win Friends and Influence the Habits of Highly Effective People?* Give me a break."

"I'm serious. They will change your life. All you do is flounder. You need to set some *goals*. Read some Dale Carnegie or Earl Nightingale. Or Stephen Covey: he's pretty amazing."

Gab nodded his head.

"Okay, jeez—I'll read all of them if you just relax and sit here next to me. You always do this. When we go to the movies, you have to sit a seat over from me, because God forbid people might think something . . . you big homophobe."

"That's not why. It's because the popcorn goes in the seat between us. Otherwise we'd be groping for it in someone's lap. Ugh. Why do I even bother arguing with you?"

A waitress came over. Gab always wondered why the waitresses at this place were so damn ugly. He could swear they all got hired coming straight out of a methadone clinic.

The waitress looked suspiciously at the two men sitting practically in each other's lap.

"Umm . . . Hi there," she said. "What can I get you two to drink?"

"There's gum on the other side of the booth," Pal hurriedly explained. "That's why we are both sitting here. We're not together like that. Not that there's anything wrong with that, but we're not."

"Thanks for setting me straight," she deadpanned. "Want me to get you another booth?"

Gab flicked a wrist at her.

"Don't even think about it. This spot just *surges* with energy," he said, doing t'ai chi movements with his arms. Pal slapped them down.

"You know what?" said the waitress. "I hear Patrick Swayze came in here once and waited for this booth for thirty minutes. Something about energy, too. That was back before he became a movie star, you know, when he lived out here in Deepwater. I know someone who used to work here that used to date him. That was a long time ago, though."

Gab gave Pal an I-told-you-so look.

"I knew it! Swayze's the man. So spiritual."

"He is not."

"He so is. Haven't you seen *Roadhouse*? That movie is filled with all kinds of Eastern philosophy. Remember that line, 'Pain don't hurt'? Come on! How much more Zen can you get?"

"I love that movie," said the waitress.

"He is not spiritual!" said Pal, clearly exasperated. "That was just a character he was playing!"

"Ssh, not so loud, honey," said the waitress. "There are a lot of seniors here this time of night. They get startled easily."

"Senior citizens? At one a.m.?" Pal looked around. "We're the only ones here besides that one old fart over there, and he looks like he's stone deaf."

"Hey now, be nice. He doesn't go around making snap judgments about people like *you*, does he?" the waitress said.

"People like *me*?!"

"She's right, Pal," said Gab, who had a healthy habit of siding with the person who could potentially spit in his food.

The waitress gleamed at him.

"Now, can I get you two lovebirds some juice or bottled water?"

"Coffee. Black," Pal said. "And we're not gay!"

As the waitress left, shaking her head, the old man sitting a few tables over got up and shuffled past Pal and Gab toward the restroom.

"Sure," the old man muttered as he passed their booth.

"You want trouble, old timer?" Pal said.

"What are you going to do, climb over your boyfriend and kiss me?" the old man chuckled.

"Calm down fellas," Gab said, playing peacemaker. "Sorry about that, sir."

The old man shook the tip of his well-weathered cane at them.

"You got nothing to apologize for. Your boyfriend, on the other hand, better mind his manners, or he's going to get my foot so far up his ass he'll be tasting my aglets."

Gab winced.

"Aglets?" asked Pal.

"That's them little thingies on the tips of shoelaces, to stop them from unraveling. They're called aglets."

"Ah."

"Yeah."

The old man resumed his trek to the restroom. Gab and Pal watched him go in silence. It took him a minute to cover ten feet of ground. The silence dragged on.

"Jesus, Pal! What's wrong with you?" Gab asked as the restroom door closed again.

Pal kept staring at the door. Gab had only seen an old man having trouble walking to the john, but Pal had seen fifty years into the future, when he would be old and alone.

He had not told Gab about how his fiancée had slid the ring across the table to him at the furniture store a week prior, or about the panic attack he had after coming back to a gutted apartment. Pal still had the ring in his pocket. He did not know why he carried it around.

He took it out and put it on the table in front of them. Gab stared at it.

"Not that I'm not flattered," he mumbled. "But I'm honestly only sitting with you here because of the gum on the other side."

"She called it off, Gab. She gave me back the ring and left me. And then she cleaned out our place. You should see it right now. It's . . . so empty it's huge."

"Oh, shit. Look, I'm sorry, man. I had no idea. Fuck this. Let's get out of here before Colonel Potter over here feeds your ass his shoelace thingies."

A waitress came up to Gab sitting alone in the booth. She was quite attractive. This made Gab even more sad. Everything was changing.

"Can I get you something to drink, honey?" she said.

"Yes. Two coffees, please."

"Expecting someone?" she said with all of her teeth. She had a gorgeous smile.

Gab closed his eyes for a moment.

"No. Just an old habit," he answered. "One coffee. Black."

|EPILOGUE| June 2007

# Chapter 31

Gab's desk was clean, tidy, and had a framed picture of Gab and Bovary in the corner. They were in London, in front of the Tate Modern, standing cheek to cheek and smiling through the cold wind blowing off the Thames. The fellow tourist who snapped the picture had taken them for newlyweds.

One of Gab's students entered, plopped a heavy gift on the desk, and took his seat next to the star lineman of the football team. The star lineman commented on the weight of "that heavy-ass mother": he had been the one who carried it around the whole first half of the day.

Gab walked in, dressed as always to the nines in a corduroy blazer with suede elbows, nicely pressed chinos, and an oxford shirt. He had made a promise to himself that he would always dress nicely in his new profession, and in three years he had not strayed from this promise—not even on "Spirit Fridays," when teachers were allowed to wear school T-shirts and jeans. It was the last day of the year and his last day as a high school teacher. He could have worn shorts if he had wanted to, but he chose not to break with his own tradition.

Gab looked at the package on his desk. The wrapping paper was wrinkled all to hell, and the big bow on top of the box had seen better days.

"Well now, what's this, a gift for the teacher? Am I in the right classroom?"

"We got you a going-away present," said Lauren. Gab noticed that, once again, she was not dressed according to school dress code, sporting a low-cut blouse that exposed the top of a black lace bra. Gab decided to let it go this time. In a little over an hour, she would be off campus and entering a new world where she would be breaking the hearts of college boys and probably those of a few professors as well.

"We're still mad at you for selling out, though," piped up Chelsea. "Open it, open it!"

"Okay, okay," Gab said as he opened the present. "Hey! Well how about that! You guys, this is so cool."

It was a very old and very dusty typewriter.

"It's an Underwood Portable from the '30s," said Chance. "I stole it from my parents' antique shop."

"Aren't they going to miss it?"

"That thing has been in the store ever since me and Chance were kids," said Daniel, his twin. Gab disliked him. "We used to bang on the keys. By the way, the F key is screwed up. And three others: U, C, and one other . . ."

"K?" suggested Gab.

"No, the back space. Anyway, we wanted to give it to you, since you taught us how to write . . . or at least tried to. You did the best you could, I guess."

"Well, I'll write my next play on this typewriter. I guess I'll keep it PG-13, without too many F words. I'll make sure to blame it on you guys in the dedication."

"What's it going to be about? Being a hotshot writer living in New York City, drinking lattes all day?" Chelsea asked.

"As if I can afford the rent in Manhattan. I've only got one play produced so far, and it's so off-Broadway, it's in Brooklyn."

"Well, don't let the critics give you as much shit as we did," said the star lineman.

"Language, Jeremy," said Gab out of habit.

Officially, the students were required to take a final exam, but as this was an elective creative writing course, Gab told them to use the last five minutes of class to write the worst opening sentence to a novel they could think of. The only one still in her seat after the bell had rung was Olesya, an exchange student from the Ukraine.

"Well, what are you waiting for?" Gab asked her after the other students hustled out. "Get out of here. It's officially summer break."

"I don't know. I'm not sure if I like my sentence," she said.

"You're not supposed to like it. It's supposed to be terrible. Ah, never mind. You get an A plus," Gab said. "Go, enjoy your summer."

She thanked him and handed him her piece of paper as she left. Gab read her sentence.

"Although honestly, it should be an F," he said to himself. "This is an awfully good opening line."


Gab was entering the final grades into the computer when Bovary walked in the classroom. She had her hair pulled up in a knot and wore designer frames and a well-tailored suit that must have complemented her backside quite nicely—Gab noticed the assistant principal admiring it as he showed Bovary in.

"Bov!" Gab jumped up and hugged his former business partner.

"Hey, teach. You are too cute for words. Look at you."

He hugged her once more. "So good to see you! What are you doing here?"

The last time Gab had seen Bovary was in London four years earlier, driving away in a cab toward Gatwick. She was moving to Dallas to manage an erotic boutique, and he was finishing up his master's degree in education. They had decided that they needed to get away on the year anniversary of Pal's death, so on a whim they flew to England together. It was the best time they had since the tragedy. Being across an ocean from Texas helped.

"Well," Bovary said after the long embrace. "I thought it only proper to drive down here and see you off after reading that e-mail you sent out of the blue. You never call, you never write, and when you do, you drop some major shit. When are you leaving?"

"Tomorrow, actually. I have the car packed and everything."

"Well, looks like I came just in time. Did you sell the house?"

"Yeah, the equity can cover my rent and expenses for while. I got a cheap place in Queens. An ex-girlfriend who lives up there hooked me up. Her day job is finding apartments for people, so that was convenient. Got me a great deal."

"Any romance brewing?" Bovary asked.

Gab shook his head and blushed. Bovary couldn't remember him being so shy.

"No, not at all. I started talking to her here and there after everything calmed down. We've become really good friends, but nothing else."

"You really are something," Bovary said. Gab had aged slightly since she'd seen him last, but in a good way. He was beginning to get crow's feet, probably from his way of laughing with squinted eyes, which made her smile.

"Here," she said, handing him a magazine. "I guess I have another reason for coming to see you."

Gab looked at the odd publication. The cover was a photograph of two dogs, one shaved and with a cone around its neck, the other holding a red ball in its mouth.

"*Art Bitch?* What is this?"

"Look on page thirty-three," Bovary said. "The ad in the lower right-hand corner."

The small advertisement had a photograph of a peculiar still life: an orchid splattered with bright red paint.

"My God," he said, pulling the small ad in for a closer look. "Is this for real?"

"It is. It's her stuff. She's exhibiting in a gallery in Brooklyn. You'll be up there by that time. There's no reason why you can't go to the opening."

"She moved to New York?"

"I'm only authorized to tell you about the exhibit. We were in touch recently. But I can tell you that she'll be there on that night."

"I can't go."

"I bet she'd love to see an old friend. You should swing by, say hello."

"I can't."

Gab gave the magazine back to Bovary, who placed it on his desk between the typewriter and the photograph.

"Well, give it some thought. While you do, we are going to get out of here and get shit-faced. The dive bars here are so much better than in Dallas."

Gab laughed. Shit-faced sounded pretty good to him.

"Afterwards, will you take me home and molest me with something spiky and rubbery? For old times' sake?" he asked.

"Sure," said Bovary. "Good thing I brought my travel-sized gear."

# Chapter 32

V'Lacke Bos Gallery — Park Slope, Brooklyn, New York

It was late, and the crowd of people pestering Marisa with questions was beginning to thin. Her paintings were a big hit. A critic from *Art Bitch* was effusive in his praises, which heralded good things for the next issue. He called her work "menstruation in bloom." In any other publication, this review would sound the death knell of her career. Coming from *Art Bitch*, it was going to cement her reputation as a to-be-contended-with artist.

The first thing that Gab noticed about her was that she did not seem as surprised as he had anticipated.

"Hello, Marisa," he said. The people around her were so loud he wondered if she had heard him.

"Gab," she said. Her entourage stared at him. "Guys, please excuse me for a moment."

They left her circle of admirers behind and walked to a quiet corner of the gallery. She held onto his arm and felt a slight tremble.

"Didn't expect me?" he asked.

"Bovary e-mailed me. She said you might show." The conversation started slowly. The two had quite a history but none of a recent nature.

"I like your stuff. Where did you get the idea for these paintings?" Gab asked.

"From a visionary," Marisa answered.

"Well, he must be something. Handsome, too, I bet," Gab said.

"He's okay," Marisa said and left him to admire a canvas full of vibrant clouds of color and bold curves while she went to the bar.

"I'm glad you're here," she said after coming back with two beers.

"Bovary told me about the show. Saw it in a magazine."

"I mailed it to her. *Art Bitch* doesn't circulate in Texas yet. She told me about your play. And that you were moving to New York. Congratulations."

"I didn't know you two kept in touch."

"Off and on," Marisa said. "Look at us. No one would believe this, us meeting again on this side of the country. It's gotta be fate."

Gab wondered if Bovary had pushed for this reunion or if it was all Marisa's idea. Either way, he didn't dwell on it. He didn't have to come to this gallery. He didn't have to ride the F train for an hour and get lost for another hour trying to find the place. If it was destiny, he had certainly given it plenty of assistance.

"Look, um, I've been wanting to say this. I'm sorry I kicked you out of my life so abruptly. I realize you were trying to comfort me when Pal died, and I had no right to treat you like that," Gab said.

"You had every right. And as I recall, I was the one who ended things between us. Let's face it: we were no good for each other. Not back then."

"Maybe," he said and took a big swig of his beer.

"I want to show you something." Marisa led him across the loft and up to a huge expanse of newly painted sheetrock with a solitary small painting hanging in its center. It was the orchid Gab had splattered with red paint—the one she had used for her ad in the art magazine.

"I took a few years off, but I finally finished the collection. And this is where it all started."

"How much is this one?" Gab asked.

"It's not for sale."

Gab stared at the painting. It brought back everything, both the good and the terrible.

"How's married life?" he asked, still staring at the painting.

Marisa looked around for something.

"I'm divorced," she said, looking back at Gab.

"Sorry," Gab said.

"Don't be," Marisa said. 'We tried, but . . ." She looked around once more. "Stay there. I want to show you something else."

"Right," he said under his breath.


As soon as Marisa walked away, Gab reached up and took the painting from the wall. The remaining people in the gallery were either too drunk or too preoccupied, so no one saw him tuck the painting under his arm and walk out the front door.

Marisa returned to the place where Gab had been standing. Both he and the painting were gone.

The little girl standing beside Marisa tugged at her hand.

"Mommy, I want to go now," she said.

Marisa bent down and picked up the tired child.

"In a little bit, baby. I just . . ." Marisa looked around once more, shook her head slightly, and smiled. "Never mind, sweetie. Let's go. Mommy will order room service. You like room service, don't you?"

"Yes," the girl said quietly, resting her head on her mother's shoulder.


Waiting for the F train that would take him back to Queens, Gab stood next to a man playing an old Martin guitar. There were only a handful of people on the platform, yet the man played and sang with his whole heart and soul.

"Do you take requests?" Gab asked him when his song was over, dropping twenty dollars into the man's guitar case. The musician smiled an appreciative smile.

"Nope. Just US currency."

Gab grinned as the guitarist played a twelve-bar blues chord progression and sang in a gruff baritone:

> Your baby done whipped ya
> Your baby done shamed ya

*Your baby done talking, she don't know your name but*
*You will believe in love*
*You better hope your baby change her mind*
*Before you, you in the sky above*
*You better do the things that's on her mind so you,*
*You will believe in love . . .*

# Chapter 33

Gab's Apartment – Astoria, Queens, New York

At his apartment, Gab placed Marisa's painting on the dining room table and pulled up a chair. After examining it for a minute or two, he rubbed his eyes and started to sniffle.

"Dena, are you down there?" he asked, looking beneath the table. He scooted his chair back to let the large Hemingway cat jump up on his lap.

Sneezing violently a couple of times, he pulled out a folded piece of paper from his shirt pocket. He had been memorizing the sentence written on it. It was Olesya's final exam response, the worst opening sentence to a novel she could think of. Gab read it aloud to Dena, who could care less.

"The average bear, by nature a quadruped, can skip."

|END|

# |THANK YOU|

To my family, friends, and fellow writers: you know who you are, and I am grateful for the support you all (y'all) have given me throughout the years.

And to my editor, Anna Zaigraeva, who helped me tremendously and challenged me to be a better writer. You are a true talent, and this book would not be what it is without your keen eye.